"Sheriff." I looked to see who said that because the tone of voice wasn't that of a warning. It was the scruffy one who'd been holding the shotgun earlier. He inclined his head in my direction and added, "He's awake."

One of the others finished his coffee and tossed the dregs onto the ground while he peered at me. After a moment he came to my side, where he stood looming over me. "Are you hungry?" he asked. "Would you like some coffee?"

Neither question was exactly what I would have expected. "Who are you?" I asked. "And what do you want with me?"

"A fair enough question. I'm Sheriff John Merlin of Lewis County in the sovereign state of Nevada. These men have been deputized as a posse. I can assure you that our capture of you is entirely legal. Does that satisfy your curiosity?"

"Who are you chasing?"

Sheriff John Merlin smiled gently. "No one. Not now."

I can be slow sometimes. It finally dawned on me. . . . "You think I'm the person you're after, don't you? Sheriff, I'm sorry to tell you this, but you've gone to a great deal of trouble for nothing. You have the wrong man in custody. I'm innocent."

The smile grew all the broader. "D'you know, son, those are words I've heard before. . . ."

LEWISVILLE FLATS

FRANK RODERUS

LEISURE BOOKS NEW YORK CITY

A LEISURE BOOK®

September 2002

Published by

Dorchester Publishing Co., Inc.
276 Fifth Avenue
New York, NY 10001

ISBN: 0-8439-5026-9

Visit us on the web at www.dorchesterpub.com.

LEWISVILLE FLATS

One

Chapter One

The world was mine, or so I felt in the late winter of '82. Opportunity lay before me without boundary that year because, you see, my uncle Edward chose me to buy our horses for the spring work.

Apart from the honor of the assignment and aside from the fact that I embrace responsibility the way ruffians and ne'er-do-wells embrace bawdy women, I considered this to be an excellent omen for the future. Uncle Edward, you should understand, has only daughters, and it has been understood ever since Aunt Ethel stopped conceiving that one of us nephews would inherit responsibility for the Bar X Bar. Not ownership, of course, but operating control, which in my mind is by far the more important of the two.

You have probably heard of the Bar X Bar, for it is the largest ranch in all of northern Nevada. You probably have not, however, heard of me.

My name is Boyd Little, although some call me Big. Because I am. This seems to amuse them. I do not know why.

Our procedure for some years has been to buy horses in the south each winter so we would have grass-fat stock available to us at the earliest possible date. The grazing matures much later in the north, and it always takes free-ranging horses a considerable amount of time to recover their weight and strength after the poorer feed of winter.

By selling off all but a necessary few saddle horses each fall and buying fresh mounts again in the early spring, we are able to get a jump on the other ranchers' roundups and have our steers to market at the earliest possible moment when supplies are still low in the east and prices are at their highest.

Uncle Edward devised this strategy years ago, and it has served the family well. Until this year, however, Uncle Edward always took personal charge of the annual horse buying.

The fact that he was entrusting me with the job this year was both an honor and a thrill, and it was my earnest desire to prove his faith in me well-founded. And never mind what my cousins might think or say or do.

I rode out from the Bar X Bar, therefore, with a glad heart and a firm resolve, my favorite bay horse under me. And three thousand four hundred dollars in gold coin secreted between the horse and myself. I had, you see, taken some pains to conceal the money, placing some inside the curve of the saddle tree and sewing the remainder of the horse fund inside the lining of the saddle skirts.

I quite frankly would have been more comfortable had Uncle Edward allowed me to carry a letter of credit to pay for the horses, but he, prudent and frugal soul that he is, made me understand that a seller will be far more impressed by the yellow of coin than the white of paper and can thus be lured into a lower price for specie than for any form of note or promise.

Uncle Edward was, I was sure, entirely correct about this.

And as I believe I have mentioned, responsibility is no burden to me.

I therefore at the age of thirty-two kissed my mother and my father, shook hands with each of my cousins and with

4

a pledge to Uncle Edward that I would return with my shield or upon it—figuratively speaking, that is—set forth on what would prove to be the most fateful journey of my life.

Chapter Two

It felt funny to be off on my own like that. Strange, but kind of exciting too.

The truth was, I'd never been much of anyplace before. The farthest I'd ever been from home was down to the railroad at Kyne Springs, where we took our steers for shipping each year, and that wasn't but twenty-seven or-eight miles. Two easy days driving the beeves and one day to ride home again. And even then I doubt I was ever much more than an arm's reach away from one cousin or another. I'd sure never been anyplace exciting, and never anyplace at all alone.

Riding two, three hundred miles with no company but my own was something new and very different.

The sky seemed somehow wider and the land bigger once I was out of sight from the roofs of the Bar X Bar, where practically everybody I knew in this whole world remained.

Even the horse under me seemed to feel it, tossing his head and snorting and in general forgetting his manners so that I had to spin him around in some whirligig circles one way and then the other to take a little of the sass out of him

and put his mind to business. He rode easier after that. I
can't say that I did. I was still marveling at the strangeness.

It was . . . a free feeling. If that makes sense. I had a responsible job to do and was out on my own to do it how
and where I thought best.

Uncle Edward made that clear enough. If I could find
horses that I liked in the Meadows, that was fine. I could
buy them, hire my crew, and start back then and there. If I
didn't like what I found there I could go on down into Mexico, east into Arizona, all the way over to California if that's
what I favored. I could do it however I wanted, just so I
had seventy-five head of strong, fat, ready-to-work saddle
stock back on the Bar X Bar in time for the spring working.

And of course if I could strike a canny deal and save the
family some money, that would be an extra tall feather in
my cap.

Uncle Edward hadn't come out and said that, but I expect
I ought to know my own uncle and I knew it was the way
he would look at things. Uncle Edward believes strong in
the dictum "waste not, want not". Scotsmen have been
known to come to him for lessons in frugality. So if I could
make a good bargain, that would strengthen my jump on
the cousins for the job of running the Bar X Bar some fine
day.

I was thinking about that sort of thing when I rode into
the town limits of Kyne Springs late in the forenoon of that
first day and passed clean on through. Wasn't even tempted
to stop there for a celebratory beer or two or a meal. I
walked the big bay slow over the railroad tracks and around
the loading chutes and completely ignored the town and its
attractions. There'd be no sowing of wild oats for me,
thank you. This trip was pure business, and I wanted to get
about it.

A bit of breeze sprang up from the east as I was passing
by, and for a moment there I could hear the tinkling of a
player piano and thought I could smell a whiff of French
perfume. That was probably sheer imagination, though, and
I ignored all of that and stretched the bay into a smooth
road walk that would put the miles behind without unduly

taxing his stamina. After all, this journey was only beginning and we had a long, long way yet to go.

I was completely ready for whatever might come.

I thought.

Chapter Three

Nevada is laid out so that it's easy as pie to travel north or south but a powerful nuisance if a body were to want to go east or west.

I've always imagined that if there was a mountain peak tall enough for you to see the whole thing all at once, it would look sort of like the bellows fabric on a concertina or an accordion—all long valleys separated by row upon row of knife-ridged mountains.

If you want to ride north to south or vice versa, all you need do is pick yourself a valley and go. There won't be much of anything in the way to hinder if that's the way your travel takes you.

East to west, of course, is a whole different kettle of fish. The flats are easy enough to cross, but you would have to work plenty hard to find your way over, through, or around one nasty little mountain range after another. If you don't already know your way, it could be pretty uncomfortable.

Lucky for me, I was going north to south and didn't have to fret about that and luckier still in that Kyne Springs and the Bar X Bar lie pretty much straight north from the place

9

called the Meadows, which is where Uncle Edward expected me to find the horses we needed.

And if that didn't work out, the Meadows was where the old California Road passed through, running all the way from the Mississippi River to the Pacific Ocean. I could follow that road one direction or the other if I chose to.

The one thing I was already convinced of was that I would *not* be going the rest of the way south into Mexico. It's one thing to wander alone in the states and territories of a body's own natural-born country, but I sure didn't want to find myself surrounded by a bunch of foreigners who couldn't even speak English. That would be a bit much, thank you.

Anyway, I rode along happy as a hog in a wallow those first few days out from home.

Mama had packed plenty of eatables to keep me happy, and of course I'd done my share of camp cooking ever since I was old enough to build a cow-chip fire and slice bacon into a spider. All of us boy cousins were taught horses, cows, and the basics of how to get along in open country, just like all the girls in the family learned to be ladies in the parlor and artists in the kitchen. I didn't go hungry.

And I discovered a particular joy once I was out by myself like that.

I could sing.

Loud as I liked.

And there wouldn't be anybody groaning or cussing or begging for me to quit.

I have, I will confess, what is probably the awfulest, scratchiest, most thoroughly vexatious voice in all of Nevada. Maybe in all the country. The just plain worst. And believe me, I have this on very good authority, for pretty much everybody who's ever heard me sing has given me this same piece of information.

Sometimes at night when circling a bunch of cows I used to sing to them soft and low. Crooning, like. I had to quit doing it, though, and leave the gentling voices to other nightherders, for even the cows refused to abide my voice and got spooky.

The pity of it is that I do so very dearly love to sing. Sometimes I'll top a rise and see a mirage shimmering in the distance or come quiet into a glade and spot a doe with a pair of spotted fawns at her side or look on an especially colorful sunset and the feeling inside me will just beg to burst out in song.

Singing gladdens my soul in a way few other things do, and on the half-dozen or so occasions when we've had a circuit-riding preacher close enough to listen to, for me the best part of the meeting was always when the folk got to singing. My cousins couldn't shush me if we were singing in services, you see, so I could just rear back and let 'er roar.

And now, riding alone miles and miles away from any ears but those of my own horse, I was able to sing to my heart's content.

I'd sing until I got hoarse, wet my whistle a mite, and sing some more. I loved it.

I was still enjoying the novelty of it when I reached the Big Marsh. Which, of course, I'd heard about for pretty near as long as I could remember. I'd never expected to see it myself, but right there it was. A swamp. There in the middle of the sage and alkali flats that filled this valley I was riding through. Dangedest thing I ever did see. It struck me so much that I stopped singing and just sat there on the back of the bay looking out over the marsh and marveling at the sight of it.

It was almost like a long, narrow lake, except shallow and with cattails and grasses growing up past the surface of the gray and kind of scummy-looking water. It too ran north and south, so it wouldn't really present a barrier to me as I could just ride around one side or the other and be on about my way.

Back in the days of the emigrants, though, and of the Pony Express after them, the Big Marsh had been a huge problem, for the bottom wasn't hard enough to drive a loaded wagon across without bogging axle deep. Nor solid enough to run a horse through, either, without risking a broken leg.

The wagons making their way west to California would

11

Frank Roderus

have to unload nearly empty and the folks carry their things piggyback the whole way across the marsh to the west side. I guess an awful lot of the heavier things got left behind on the east side for lack of any way to get them across.

I was about half tempted to ride around on the east side of the marsh just to see if there were yet any pianos or trunks or whatnot still sitting there in the hot, dry air.

But there was a place of historic interest on the west side that fascinated me even more, and that was where there'd once been a genuine Pony Express way station, one of the many that joined St. Jo, Missouri, at the east end of the pony riders with San Francisco on the west.

Oh, I'd read about the pony boys. All my life. And big though I am and heavy on the back of even a stout horse, when I was a boy I would sometimes imagine myself riding fast and proud. Being chased by wild Indians. Riding through rain and snow and storm. Riding into whirlwinds. Facing danger but never slowing, never flinching.

I suppose all boys dream like that. Now, I was a long way from being a boy. But the Pony Express . . . the stories of those riders still thrilled me.

If there was the smallest chance that I could stop now and visit what was left of an actual, honest-to-Pete Pony Express station . . .

I reined the bay to take him around on the west side of the Big Marsh.

Chapter Four

"And it's all for me grog, me jolly jolly grog, all for me beer and tobacco."

Whoever was singing—it seemed hard to believe—but I really thought his voice was even worse than mine. Incredible.

"Well, I spent all me tin on the lassies drinkin' gin. Across the wide ocean I'll wander.

"I'm sick in the head and I haven't gone to bed since I first came ashore from me slumber. For I've spent all me dough on the lassies don't you know. Far across the wide ocean I'll wa-a-a-a-an-der.

"And it's all for me grog, boys, me jolly jolly grog, all for me beer an' toBAcco. Well I spent all me tin on the LASSIES drinkin' gin. Across the wide ocean I'll WANder."

I heard somebody laugh and then some scraping and stamping that I took to be the sound of somebody dancing. Or perhaps . . . actually I wasn't sure what was going on over on the other side of the half-fallen wall of what must once have been a Pony Express relay station.

Whatever was going on inside what remained of the shel-

13

ter, the parties there were certainly of the opinion that they were alone. I felt more than a trifle embarrassed to have sneaked up on them like this and brought my horse to a quick halt a dozen or so paces from what was left of the old structure.

"Hello," I called out. "Is anybody there?"

The scuffling sounds stopped abruptly and a head poked out past the door frame.

All I could see was the face, but that was enough. The fellow looked for all the world like the drawing of a leprechaun I'd seen in a book once upon a time. Flaming-red hair. Round, apple cheeks. Impishly turned-up nose. And above all else, a wide and beaming gap-toothed smile.

Then the fellow stepped outside—well, outside was a relative term, as there was no roof remaining, although a good three quarters of the front wall still stood and the now-empty door frame—and the leprechaun impression was reinforced. He couldn't have stood more than five feet and small change. Probably would've had to use a stepping stool to meet his own reflection eye to eye in a mirror.

"Faith now!" he exclaimed with a grin. "It's salvation ye bring me, son, just as me prayers requested."

I squinted down at him with, I will admit, no small degree of skepticism. "Forgive me for saying so, but you don't look like my idea of a priest."

This for some reason caused the little fellow to throw his head back and roar loudly enough that I shortened my rein lest the bay take fright.

"A praist, is it? Ye're askin' if I am a praist? Lord love ye, son, but ye've a sweet sense o' humor, ye have."

"I do?" This was not something anyone had accused me of in the past. I rarely jested, and of course hadn't been this time either.

"It's no praist I be, but simple Liam O'Day of County Armagh in God's own green land."

"I didn't mean to interrupt," I explained. "I was passing by and heard . . . well, actually, I'd come this way deliberately so I could see this Pony Express station . . . but I heard you, um, singing."

"Ah, yes. Came from the narth, did ye?"

"Yes, I did."

"An' t' think, son,'twas from the south I was expectin' salvation."

I did not understand why he kept referring to me as "son." I had no way to be certain, of course, but suspected that Liam O'Day was younger than me by half a dozen years or more. "Salvation, you said?"

"Aye, lad, it's savin' me that brought you here. My old harse died, don't you see. Over there." He pointed toward the reeds that clogged the fringes of the alkaline bog that filled the center of this flat.

I couldn't see anything of a dead horse in all that, but there certainly was a flurry of excitement among a squawking horde of magpies a hundred or so yards south of the way station ruins. That was sure to be the spot he meant, even though it wasn't exactly the direction he'd indicated.

"Ran him too hard, did you?"

"Aye, I expect I may've," little Liam said, remorse thick in voice and expression alike. He took a deep breath and sighed. Then brightened considerably as he motioned toward the interior of the station. "Now that ye've saved me, son, won't ye also join me? Feedin' you is the least I can do in recompense for your dear an' thoughtful kindness."

I stepped down off the bay and stood there, towering head and shoulders—quite literally—above the wee fellow. We really should have traded names, I thought, as he was the one who truly was little.

Chapter Five

Liam O'Day's intentions exceeded his abilities by a rather wide margin. That is to say, he was openhanded and cheerful in his offer of hospitality. The only drawback was that he had nothing to offer but tea, which he carried in a tin box.

"Me goods, don't ya see, the flour an' meal an' the like, was all ruint by that nasty-tastin' water when me harse fell doon."

"Bad-tasting, you said?"

"Aye,'tis perfec'ly awful stuff, I'm tellin' ye."

"You haven't been drinking it, have you?"

He pointed toward the enameled pot that seemed to be his primary and perhaps only cooking utensil. "Makes even honest tay taste turrible, I'm tellin' ye."

I went over to the coals of his smokeless little fire, picked up the pot, and with a flip of my wrist sent the gyp-water tea out the empty doorway.

"What'd ya do a thing like that for, me son?"

"That water won't do much worse than give you a good bellyache and maybe a case of the runs. Well, not unless

16

you drink an awful lot of it. I'm not sure how bad it would be if you did that. But I wouldn't drink any more of it if I were you."

Liam's eyes grew all the bigger in his freckled face, and he clutched at his belly as if to determine if it had begun to hurt without him noticing quite yet.

"I'm afraid the leaves were ruined. But I can get you some good water if you want to boil more."

"Water, son? Where'd ye be findin' water other'n what's out there?" He pointed toward the rushes where his horse's carcass was still pleasing the magpies.

"There will be a spring or a seep somewhere close by. Has to be or why else would they put this relay station here?"

"Had'na thought o' that, had I?"

"Wait here." I took Liam's rather battered pot and went outside. The spring was around back of the station, of course, as was only logical. I washed the pot out—it needed it—and refilled it. And did some awestruck looking about at the same time.

A Pony Express station. The real thing, this was. I'd read about the Express and the marvelous young men who rode for it. Now I was standing at the same spot where they once stood, brave and reckless and resolute. I wished . . .

I shook my head and gave over such silly meandering. I had much more important things to do.

But being here thrilled me just the same.

I took the pot back to Liam, then excused myself and went out to the patient bay. It was late enough in the day that there was no sense in riding on at this point. Better to spend the night here, then tomorrow I could resume my journey south.

The bay was strong enough that it would scarcely notice little Liam's weight riding double.

I took the horse around back to the water, then hobbled it and turned it loose to browse at the succulent greenery that was growing close around the little spring where the Pony Express riders once watered their horses too.

I could see where there'd once been a fairly large corral

on the sloping ground leading up onto the mountain to the west—there would be a pass up there that the Express riders must have used, although I could not see it from down here—but the adobe corral walls had melted 'most away over the years of neglect. The horse wouldn't go anywhere in hobbles, though.

I turned him loose to fill his belly, then carried my saddle and other truck inside. Liam might not have anything in the way of food to share, but I did. Between his tea and my groceries I figured we could put together a fine enough meal.

And we'd be eating it on the same spot where the Pony Express riders once did. I considered whether if by looking around I might determine exactly what functions each part of the old building had. For certain sure I intended to try.

It was with a heart as light as Liam's that I returned to the ruins.

Chapter Six

"She drove a wheelbarrow thru streets broad an' narrow, singing COCKLES an' MUSSELS, alive alive-o."

"Bringing in the sheaves, bringing in the sheaves, we will go rejoicing, bringing in the sheaves."

"An' it's all for me grog, boys, me jolly jolly grog, all for me beer an' toBACco."

"Camptown races, five miles long, doo-dah, doo-dah."

"Well, I've spent all me tin on the lassies drinkin' gin."

"Tenting tonight, tenting tonight, tenting on the old camp ground."

"Cockles an' mussels, alive alive-o, crying COCKLES an' MUSSELS, alive alive-o."

Come sundown, we sat beside that fire singing up a storm for hours and hours practically.

Liam's voice was as bad as mine, and it turned out that he loved singing just as much as I do. So we sang. Loud as we could. Well, when we weren't laughing we were singing. For as much as either one of us enjoyed singing, and never mind how bad we were at it, we couldn't either one of us remember the words to a whole song, hardly.

Which is something I've noticed more than once before. People who have the gift of song, folks whose voices are sweet and pure and true, they also seem to get the gift of being able to remember the words to those songs.

Why, I've known some—my Uncle Thomas's younger daughter Ella comes to mind first off—who have voices like angels and who can sing a whole evening through without ever having to repeat a song nor once stumbling over the words. They know the words to dozens upon dozens of songs. Heck, maybe to hundreds.

There are people like that and others who may not remember songs, but they can recall the punch lines to about every joke they've ever heard. Me, I can't keep track of either one.

Neither could Liam O'Day. Which did not stop us. Not in the slightest. What little we did remember we practically shouted.

Something else we learned, though, after discussing my observations about folks who could sing and remember words, was that of the snatches of this song and that that we did know . . . they weren't the same songs.

Liam being Catholic Irish and me being Protestant American, the one of us hadn't any experience with the songs of the other.

Which did not stop us from rearing back and letting them out. A phrase here. A chorus there. Turn and turn about.

Our bellies were full and the tea can was steaming in the cool night air. Firelight reflected off the adobe walls of the old Pony Express station. And the night was filled with song.

"Danny Boy, the pipes the pipes are calling. From glen to glen and down the mountain side."

"Amazing Grace that saved a wretch like me."

It was, I think, one of the most enjoyable evenings I'd ever had. Or at least the best I could remember right off-hand.

We were complete strangers and about as different as any two people could be, this little leprechaun of an Irishman and me. But for that one night we shared a joy that wasn't hindered by any restraints or obligations. Just let our hair down, as the old expression goes, and had a lovely time of it.

"I've been a wild rover for many's the year. An' I've spent all my money on whiskey an' beer. But now I'm returning with gold in great store, an' I never will play the wild rover no more."

No, sir, I just can't remember when I'd had an evening more fun.

Chapter Seven

I awoke to a kick in the ribs. Not a nudge. A kick. Hard.

I yelped and tried to jump upright.

Couldn't.

The twin barrels of a very large shotgun held poised over my chest prevented it.

"What the . . . ?"

"Shut up, you. Lie on your belly and put your hands behind your back." The speaker was a man with a large belly, a large mustache, and a large pair of black iron handcuffs. He was bending over me, as was the one with the shotgun.

"Who are you? What are you doing here? Where's Liam ?"

A man wearing brown corduroy trousers and dusty but otherwise very nicely kept and freshly blacked boots kicked me in the ribs beneath my right shoulder. This one was standing slightly to my rear, so his lower extremities were all I could see of him at that moment. I had to assume that he was also the one who'd kicked me while I was sleeping, as he was so quick and willing about it.

This time I did not cry out. Did not want to give these

brigands the satisfaction. Instead I swiveled around so I could get a better look at the one with the nice boots. I wanted to remember him. He had blond hair and a small, dapper mustache and wore a derby hat and bow tie.

I would remember his face. I was certain of that.

There were, I saw once I began paying attention, eight men in the group. The only one I would have taken for a ruffian had I seen any of them on a street somewhere was the one with the shotgun. That one wore rough clothing and either the beginnings of a beard or the evidence of a slothful nature, as it was clear he hadn't shaved in the better part of a week.

The rest of them, including the one with the manacles, looked more like businessmen and townspeople than itinerant robbers.

"Who are you?" I demanded again. I thought about trying to get up, but at the first hint of movement was prodded on the breastbone by the unyielding muzzles of the shotgun. I sat where I was on the bedroll my mother had sewn for me out of canvas and quilts for my twelfth birthday.

"I told you, buster. Roll over and put your hands behind your back."

"I want to know who you are and what you want," I snapped right back at him. "And don't think you can put those things on me without my consent. There may be many of you, but I warn you that I can give as good as I get and I am not afraid of you. Not singly nor all of you at once."

It was a brave speech.

It was also rather stupid.

I heard a sound like that of a ripe watermelon being whacked with a sturdy oak limb and felt a dull but *very* brief sensation at the back of my head.

I had no idea of it at the time, but someone standing out of my sight behind me had struck me—exceptionally hard—with a bludgeon of some sort.

That was the last thing I knew for some little time to come.

Chapter Eight

Headache? And then some. It felt like the back part of my head was caved in, an impression that I could not verify because my hands were firmly tethered behind my back. It seemed they'd gotten those manacles on without my consent after all.

I didn't know how long I'd been unconscious, but it was more than just a minute or two. I could tell that because a fresh fire had been built up from the coals of the fire Liam and I shared and it'd been crackling long enough to boil coffee. The scent of it was rich in my nose, and some of the men held tin cups that they drank from now and then.

The shotgun had been laid aside, but this was still a well-armed bunch. My heart sank to think that these men were going to walk off with Uncle Edward's horse money. Less than a week on the road and already I was a failure. That thought hurt considerably worse than my head did.

Somehow they must have heard about the money I was carrying, and they came after it.

My shame was not that they'd come but that they succeeded. I should have been more vigilant.

"Sheriff." I looked to see who said that, because the tone of voice wasn't that of a warning. It was the scruffy one who'd been holding the shotgun earlier. He inclined his head in my direction and added, "He's awake."

The one who had had the manacles finished his coffee and tossed the dregs onto the ground while he peered at me. After a moment he came to my side, where he stood looming over me. "You were saying something about the handcuffs?" he inquired.

"Never mind," I told him. "I gather I was wrong about that."

"So you were," he agreed, squatting closer to my level. "Are you hungry? Would you like some coffee?"

Neither question was exactly what I would have expected. But then, by now I was beginning to think my first impressions might have been just a bit wide of the mark. "Who are you," I asked, "and what do you want with me?"

"A fair enough question. I am Sheriff John Merlin of Lewis County in the sovereign state of Nevada. These men have been deputized as a posse. I can assure you that our capture of you is entirely legal. Does that satisfy your curiosity?"

"Who are you chasing?"

Sheriff John Merlin smiled gently. "No one. Now."

I can be slow sometimes. It finally dawned on me. . . . "You think I'm the person you are after, don't you?"

The sheriff's expanded smile confirmed what was only now obvious to me. These possemen did indeed believe I'd done something—I had no idea what—and were in the process of arresting me for that crime.

"Sheriff," I said, "I am sorry to tell you this, but you've gone to a great deal of trouble for nothing. You have the wrong man in custody. I'm innocent."

The smile grew all the broader. "D'you know, son, those are words I've heard before. Forgive me if I've become a skeptic."

I will admit that my heart sank.

25

Chapter Nine

I had to tell them. Had to convince them. Above all, I had to keep them from finding the gold hidden inside my saddle. Good Lord! If they found all those gold coins they would never believe I hadn't stolen them.

I had to . . . Liam. Liam could help me. He could tell them about me. We'd talked about all manner of things last night. He would . . .

Where *was* Liam, anyway?

I struggled into a sitting position that was sufficiently upright that I could at least see the inside of the old relay station.

I could see only the posse members there. They and some accoutrements that they seemed to have brought along with them. Firearms, mostly, and sacks of food and coffee and the like.

A large coffeepot was on the fire, and there was no sign now of Liam's tin pot that he made his tea in.

Where was . . . ?

My saddlebags were there where I'd put them last night, and of course I still had my bedroll. I was sitting on that.

But my saddle! Where was my saddle? Where was Uncle Edward's horse money?

I couldn't see the saddle anywhere.

If the saddle was missing . . . and if Liam O'Day was missing . . .

I then blurted out what must surely be the most stupid, unthinking, completely asinine question I have ever in my life posed.

"Sheriff," I asked, "have you seen anything of the little Irish leprechaun who was staying here with me?"

Chapter Ten

"I don't believe a word of it," the scruffy one said quite firmly. "The son of a bitch wants us to think he's soft in the head so we'll go light on him."

I had already tried to explain myself by expanding on that question. They weren't listening. I suppose in a way I can't really blame them. I mean . . . a leprechaun? Of all the dumb things to say . . .

"Sheriff, please listen to me," I pleaded. Didn't make a lick of difference, of course. Once I'd gone and as good as told them that I was at best a half-wit, there was not one single member of the posse who paid the least attention to me. They talked about me among themselves as if I weren't there.

And while the ragged one with the shotgun, whose name seemed to be Dan something-or-other, claimed that he believed I was faking foolishness, he did not really mean that. They were all, Dan included, convinced that I was soft in the head. Sly, perhaps. But not entirely there.

After all, who believes in leprechauns apart from the daft, the drunk, and the dull? And since I was demonstrably so-

28

ber, well, the remaining possibilities were limited, weren't they.

I sat there, trying not to pay attention to the posse members' self-satisfied chortlings and character assassination, and tried looking for a bright side to this. So far as I could tell . . . there wasn't one.

The longer I sat there and the more closely I inspected my surroundings, the more obvious it became to me what occurred while I was sleeping. And while this posse was creeping up on me.

At some time before the posse came onto the scene, Liam hied himself well out of it.

In a word . . . absconded.

The simple fact most assuredly had to be that while I slept, Liam took my saddle—and Uncle Edward's horse money—and crept away.

"Sheriff. Sheriff! Excuse me please. Sheriff?" I had to go on like that for some small amount of time before I was even able to get the man to turn his head in my direction.

"I'm sorry to bother you, Sheriff, but I'm worried about my horse. Have you fed and watered my horse?"

"Give it up, bub," one of the possemen said with a curse for emphasis. "You aren't gonna convince us that your horse wandered away in the night. We already found it. The magpies took us right to it."

I sighed. Liam's horse, of course.

"We got you cold, mister," another one injected. "Dan recognized the shoe on the left fore. There's a caulk missing on that shoe. Did you know that? That's more'n proof enough it's the same horse we been tracking all the way from Lewisville Flats. Any jury in the land 'd accept that for evidence."

Terrific. Not surprising, but . . . just terrific, thank you. So Liam did something in Lewisville—they hadn't yet told me what—to precipitate this little outing for the good townsfolk, then when he rode his own horse to death trying to get away, he stole mine.

Now he had my horse, Uncle Edward's money . . . and his freedom.

"What did Liam do in this Lewisville place?"

"The town is Lewisville Flats. And who is Liam?"

"Hell, Bob, Liam is an Irish name. What d'you want to bet that's the name of his leprechaun?" The comment generated a huge amount of guffawing and knee-slapping. Ignorant sons of . . . Never mind.

"Allow me to rephrase that. What happened in Lewisville . . . Flats, thank you for correcting me—what happened back there to cause your presence here?"

"That does remind me," Sheriff Merlin said. "What have you done with the money?"

"Money?" I asked.

"Don't be cute. It won't work and it only annoys us. We will find it anyway, mister, so you might as well make things easier for yourself by telling us where it is. The judge might be more lenient with you if you do."

"Believe me, Sheriff, if I knew anything about your money, I would gladly tell you. Unfortunately, I have no idea what you are talking about."

"The leprechaun did it, boys," one of them hooted, which started the hilarity all over again.

"Do as you wish," Merlin said, "but you should keep in mind that a judge and jury can hang a man for horse theft in this country. If you cooperate now, you may be able to avoid that fate later."

I think I came near to passing out when he said that. It wasn't a possibility I'd contemplated until that very moment, and I must say that it jarred me. Severely. To be convicted of a crime, particularly a crime of which I was innocent, and then *hanged* for it . . . !

Oh, how I wished I knew where they could find that foul and traitorous creature Liam O'Day. At that particular moment I believe I would've hanged the little man myself had I been able to lay hands on him, damn him.

All I could do, however, was to sit there with my hands manacled behind my back and drink deep from the bitterest dregs of regret.

Chapter Eleven

My shirt collar felt overly tight. It was not buttoned, mind, and hung free. Yet it felt constrictive. Like a noose. Swallowing did nothing to alleviate the feeling. I did not much care for the idea of being hanged to death.

Dying is one thing. We all must do it at one point or another. But to be ignominiously hanged . . . I shuddered at the thought. Literally so. I mean quite truly that I was trembling when I thought about this.

My fearful introspection was interrupted when the sheriff came to kneel beside me. I did not, I must tell you, object to his intrusion.

"I see you don't have any supplies of your own. You must be hungry."

My sack of edibles had been fairly heavy when I arrived here last night, and we hadn't eaten all that much for our supper. Obviously, Liam O'Day was eating well this morning.

The sheriff reached around behind me and tugged at the chain on my manacles, turning me half around so that I partially faced away from him.

"What I'm gonna do here, son, is take one bracelet off so I can cuff your hands in front instead. Might be best if I mention that you're a big boy and can probably account for yourself pretty well in a tussle, but you should know that there's eight of us and we aren't any one of us in a mood to wrestle or to wallow around in the dirt. If you want to make a break for it while your hands are loose, you go ahead and make your try. But we won't grab you. Dan over there will shoot you. You listening to me, son?"

I looked. The scruffy one had the shotgun in his hands again and was giving me a look that seemed kind of eager. "I'm listening, Sheriff."

"That's fine, son." The sheriff unlocked the steel clamp from my left wrist and led it around in front. I sat very still, didn't even shift position from one haunch to the other just then, and cooperatively brought my right wrist around so he could reattach the manacles in front.

I wouldn't say that Dan was disappointed, but he didn't act like he was especially relieved, either. He let the hammers down from full cock—a little detail I hadn't noticed until then—and set the shotgun down.

The first thing I did when I had that bit of regained freedom of motion was to reach up and tug at my shirt collar. That and surreptitiously rub the flesh of my neck. I could as good as feel the prickle of hemp tight around my throat.

Chapter Twelve

The sheriff was neither unfeeling nor unkind. His reason for positioning the handcuffs at my front was so I could feed myself. They brought me a meal of bacon, corn dodgers, and coffee. They did not skimp on the portions, but as stated I am larger than most and have an appetite to match. I could have had that much again and not been overly full, but I did not ask for seconds.

I was becoming more than a little annoyed with this whole situation and did not want to ask any favors from the sort of men who would come along and without so much as a by-your-leave rob me of dignity and freedom alike.

When I was done with the meal the sheriff refilled my coffee cup, then brought one of his own and sat cross-legged in front of me.

"Had enough?"

I shrugged. Like I said. No favors. I can, I will confess, be stubborn once I become set to it.

"We need to talk."

"Very well, Your Honor."

He smiled. "You'll want to call the judge 'Your honor,'

33

but I'm just the elected sheriff. You can call me 'Sheriff or you can call me 'John' or you can call my by whatever ugly cuss name seems appropriate. Believe me, it wouldn't be anything new."

"You'll have to forgive me about the protocol. This may not be new to you, but it certainly is to me."

The sheriff's smile became bigger. Quite merry, in fact. "Do you know something? You manage to say that so nicely that I could almost believe you. Except, of course, I've already seen your handiwork. Very nice. Very professional. You're good, mister. And I don't mean just when you are, shall we say, on the job. You're good at that too. But now as well. You have this bland, open, innocent expression. Like I say, I could believe you if I didn't already know so much about you." He took a swallow of the coffee and contemplated me for a moment.

I didn't say anything. But then . . . what was there to say? Deny the accusations again in the wake of those comments? It would only be a waste of breath. And breath, it seemed, was becoming more valuable to me by the moment.

"Before we go on to other things," he said after another swallow of coffee, "would you mind giving your name? We want to get it right on the records. For the indictment and trial and all."

"Boyd," I said immediately. And truthfully. And opened my mouth to add the Little.

Then I hesitated. We Littles of the Bar X Bar are a proud clan and care deeply about one another. It occurred to me that I might never see home again. Might never again enjoy the bosom of family.

And if ever they—my mother in particular, of course, but all of them in near equal measure—if ever they heard that their own entrusted Big came to meet his maker by way of a hangman's noose, it would crush them. Worse, it would humiliate them. The whole of the countryside would know, and even if the family knew better than to believe my guilt, what of those who would judge them by my supposed failings?

Better, I thought in that fleeting moment, for the family

to think I had somehow been waylaid. Better they believe that my bones lay in an unmarked scratching beside some nameless trail than for them—and all the neighbors—to know that I died the ignominious death of a felon.

Better, then, that sheriff and judge and jury know nothing of who they falsely accused.

"Bob," I quickly added.

"Boyd is the first name, then? Boyd Bob?"

"No, of course not. Boyd is the last name. Bob Boyd."

"Bob being short for Robert, I assume?"

I nodded.

"Very well, Robert Boyd. I will write it down like that." He smiled. "But I'll call you Bob, if that's all right."

"That sounds just fine to me, Sheriff," I said, meaning it. Just in case.

"Now," he said cheerfully, turning partway around and motioning for the scruffy man called Dan to join us, "there is that one other critical question I have to ask you, Bob."

"Very well."

Dan came over and walked around to stand behind me, presumably because my hands remained cuffed in front and my legs were unfettered. I could have leapt up and made a break for it had I wanted to be so rash. It pleased me slightly to note that Dan left the wicked shotgun leaning against a wall close by the fire.

"Dan, this man is Bob Boyd. And we are going to ask a few simple questions of him."

Dan grunted an acknowledgment of the statement. I remained silent.

"Bob," the sheriff said pleasantly, "please tell us where the money is."

"I'm sorry, Sheriff. I already told you. I did not commit whatever crime it is I'm accused of and I don't know where any money is." And wasn't that the unpleasant truth. I had no idea where Uncle Edward's horse money was at this moment, never mind the loot from whatever crime it was that the treacherous Liam O'Day committed to place me in this predicament.

Sheriff John Merlin sighed and gave me a look that was

both long and sorrowful. "I wish you would reconsider that statement, Bob. Please tell us where you've hidden the money."

"Truly, Sheriff, I would like to, but I really don't know. I did not do this thing you believe of me."

"As you wish, then, Bob." His eyes lifted, leaving my face and focusing somewhere behind and above me.

I heard a grunt of effort and a hissing, swishing sort of sound.

And then my back felt like a bolt of superheated lightning seared a streak of fire across it as the lash of something—a quirt, a belt, something—bit unexpected into my flesh.

I cried out and lurched forward, crashing without conscious intent into the sheriff, who continued to sit there before me.

I would suppose that they honestly believed that I was attacking him when in fact I was only reacting to the whip cut on my back.

For whatever reason—and perhaps it would have been no different had I sat docile while Dan whipped me—things became even more . . . unpleasant from that point onward.

Chapter Thirteen

Somewhere amid the pain of the whipping, I lost my sympathy for these people.

Until then, really, I'd tried to be understanding about it all, even though the simple circumstance of innocence kept me from being accommodating. After all, if I were innocent, so were they. It was Liam O'Day who committed the crime, and this group was but a duly authorized extension of law. They were in the right, and I'd felt no personal resentment at my treatment by them.

Until now.

The man called Dan enjoyed himself while he thrashed me. I know that for I could see his facial expressions clearly.

I possess, as I've already noted, my full fair share of stubbornness and then some. And this man wanted not only to wring a confession from me by brute force, he wanted to humiliate me. Wanted to break my spirit and my will.

Looking at him, the low state of his clothing, his demeanor, his person, I gathered that the other men of the posse were drawn from the prosperous and the respectable segments of society in Lewisville Flats. Dan, on the other hand, was clearly a lesser sort, no doubt brought along at a wage so as to make use of his tracking abilities.

Well, it seemed that he had abilities beyond tracking. He also knew how to inflict pain. And this he enjoyed. I could see the pleasure in his eyes as he whipped me.

His instrument of choice proved to be a rather unusual quirt fashioned with extra-long thongs. Its presence made me suspect that this particular form of amusement was not new to Dan and that he'd made his quirt with human flesh rather than equine in mind.

Once the initial shock of the assault was past, however, I would not give him the satisfaction of seeing me cringe. I came to my feet with as much dignity as I could muster and turned to face him, turning continuously so that I could look him in the eyes while he continued to wield his whip, but now having to curl it over my shoulders in order to reach the sensitive skin on my back.

Sheriff Merlin, who might have been expected to help out by holding me in place so I could not turn, stepped back instead. I could spare little time to study him at the time, but my sidelong glances lent the impression that he was studying me every bit as intently as I continued to study Dan. The sheriff made no move to join in and in fact stopped the other men of the posse from helping Dan. He let me stand, turning to present my face to Dan while I glared out all the defiance that was in me.

Had I broken and tried to attack instead . . . I do not and never will really know what might have happened in that instance, although I am sure the sheriff was quite prepared to deal with such.

I believe that just as Dan was using his lash to punish not just Boyd Little but all men who were his betters, Sheriff Merlin remained aloof so he could use this opportunity to study and assess the prisoner he knew as Bob Boyd.

As for my part of it, any sympathy I might have had for these men and their cause was quickly dissipated in the sting of Dan's quirt, and I would not have told them where to find their money even had I known, damn them.

We might have gone on like that, I suppose, until Dan's

arm became too weary to continue. Instead Dan, increasingly frustrated by my refusal to bow to the sting of the whip, stepped close with a sound much akin to a whimper and directed the leather not over my shoulder but flush on the left side of my face.

I could feel the cut of the thongs. Felt the merciful loss of sensation as that entire side of my face went instantly numb. Felt the tickling prickle of fresh blood running down my throat and into the collar of my shirt.

Without conscious thought and before any of the others could react, I reached up with my manacled hands and grasped Dan under the shelf of his jaw.

I am a more than normally large person. I would also confess to being uncommonly strong of muscle as well.

I raised my arms, and Dan found himself dangling in mid-air, legs limp with surprise, whip still in hand.

"Drop . . . the . . . quirt," I said just as slowly and as calmly as I could manage. I made no attempt to hide the fury that was in me. But I did successfully contain it.

Dan began to struggle, so I shifted my grip to put more pressure over his Adam's apple. Had I chosen to squeeze down, his windpipe would have been crushed and he would have died a slow, choking death.

"Drop . . . the . . . quirt!"

He dropped it.

I took a deep breath. Oh, I was tempted. I confess that I was sorely tempted. But I am a Little and we are a proud clan and loathe to abandon dignity. We are also not entirely stupid, and I was surrounded by seven men on whom I had *not* laid hands and would have no chance to defend myself against if they cut down on me in retaliation for whatever I might do to this miserable excuse for humanity named Dan.

"Thank you," I said with a growl.

And set the sorry son of a bitch down onto his feet again.

It was inevitable what had to follow, of course. Once Dan was free of my grasp, the remainder—save again for the sheriff himself—descended on me with their fists and their boots.

I of course expected no less—not that I would have been disappointed by the lack—and even though it probably hurt the worse and did more damage than Dan's whip, I found it in some measure more tolerable than the indignity of actual whipping.

After a time, I passed out cold and the annoyance of it went away.

Chapter Fourteen

"Hell, Jerry, just let him lay there and die. It'll be fine by me."

"Me too."

"Why wait. Go ahead and hang him now. He's half dead anyway."

Pleasant thoughts to wake up to.

"We'll have no talk of lynching." The sheriff's voice. "This is all going to be done according to law."

"Might as well hang him sooner as later, John."

"Yes, but it will be the law that hangs him, not a mob."

"He's too damned big to carry, John."

"We'll manage."

"His horse is dead an' we don't have no others."

"The two lightest can ride double until we get to the other side of the marsh. Then we'll make a travois to haul him."

And so they did.

I had no need to feign unconsciousness, especially since I was only half aware of what was going on around me anyway. I slipped in and out of that blissful state, mostly aware but as if viewing things through a dense and indeed comforting fog.

41

Frank Roderus

They draped me over the back of the largest horse in the bunch and led me across the marsh, past the bloated and stinking carcass of Liam O'Day's dead horse—no, excuse me, past the horse O'Day stole to get me in this predicament—and on to the east side of the great marsh.

There they stopped long enough to fell two small trees and rig a sturdy travois onto which they transferred me.

Then they started up the next in the endless succession of Nevada's sharp spined mountains.

I was following the old Pony Express trail, the same trail I'd dreamed of so very long ago.

Under these circumstances, I felt no thrill from it whatsoever.

Chapter Fifteen

Reaching Lewisville Flats was not pleasant. My feet were shackled together all the time and my hands were manacled behind me as well, save for the occasional purpose of eating or other, um, bodily function. Which is not an easy process when one's feet are clamped tight together.

By the time we reached the town I was one continuous ache from the nearly constant strain on my shoulders—if you do not understand that comment, have your hands tied at the small of your back and spend the next few days in this posture—and the bumping, bouncing, and jolting of the travois. And this says nothing about the lingering aches and pains left over from the drubbing they'd given me, damn them.

Any pretense of decency or consideration was abandoned and they talked over, past, and even about me as if I were an inanimate object, damn them.

It was not a comfortable trip.

By the end of the first day we'd crossed over to the east side of the one mountain, reaching the floor of yet another narrow, north–south-running valley. This they turned south into.

Late on the second day the sharp-ridged mountain to the east of that valley petered out into a series of hills and low buttes, and on the third day the valley opened wide on both sides. The eastward hills disappeared altogether, and the southern end of the mountain on the west side tailed off into foothills also and quickly disappeared so that the horizon lay almost unbroken to the south and to either side.

Lewisville Flats they'd said, and flat this land most certainly was. It was broad, barren, and dry as dust. Why anyone would choose to live here . . . Why? never mind why. *How* would be the more sensible query. The land stretched on for mile after mile with scarcely a hint of growth. Even the few thorny things that did protrude from the ground now and then had the withered appearance of dead things, although that might or might not have been so.

Naturally, from my position on the travois I could see southward only when the posse stopped for refreshment— thank goodness they seemed to have no whiskey with them, else my personal safety would have been in serious doubt— or when camped at night. If I craned my neck around, no easy task when trussed as I was, my only reward was a view of the tail and nether parts of the horse that was dragging me. I only attempted that view once.

It was roughly noon on the fourth day of travel that we arrived at the town. Four days. Liam O'Day, damn him, had given them a good run for it. Of course, he and they would have traveled considerably quicker going north than I had coming south. It was no wonder the stolen horse expired if O'Day was foolish enough to try to force it through mud and marsh at a run after so long a chase. Damn him. And them. Damn the whole blasted lot.

From my restricted view on first arrival I could see practically nothing of the town until we were actually within it. As in most small towns there was one wide, central street with businesses and a few homes ranked along both sides of it, several cross streets laid out to intersect the primary street, and a scattering of houses and other buildings all about.

I could smell but not see the presence of greenery of some

sort and came later to know that a small river starting some-where to the north and east ended here in a shallow lake before seeping into the ground at this terminus of the flow. Because of that a small grove of trees thrived, and there was water enough for the household needs of the townsfolk.

I could also hear a distant but continuous *thump-thump-thump*, as if some exceedingly heavy object were being dropped over and over and over again. This sound, noise really, was new to my experience and puzzled me.

At that moment, of course, there were other details of somewhat greater interest as my captors dragged me un-ceremoniously off the travois and into the very welcome shade of a sandstone building that turned out to be the Lewis County courthouse, including the sheriff's office and county jail.

I was, so to speak, home. Ugh.

Chapter Sixteen

I probably looked quite a sight when that same afternoon they came to fetch me for arraignment. I hadn't changed clothes for the past several very dusty and unpleasant days. I stank so bad I could smell myself. I hadn't shaved since leaving home. And while I had no mirror to look in for confirmation I assumed that I was a mass of purple bruises from the punches and kicks I'd taken. Heck, with no wash water to employ so far, I still had dried blood on me from Dan's quirt and who knows what else. I am sure I looked the part of a low ruffian.

The judge didn't look much better. In my opinion. He wore a beard and spectacles, and his face was marred by dark purple blotches. I wondered who'd kicked him around.

He also, however, wore the black judicial robe and had a small but proper courtroom to preside over.

There weren't many people present, and I gathered they'd dragged the judge away from whatever he usually did for the sole purpose of helping me along the way toward justice. Such as it was in Lewisville Flats.

The only others in the room were myself, a deputy who

looked like he should be sweeping saloon floors instead of wearing a gun and badge, and an amanuensis. A *female* amanuensis, if you can believe that. If I hadn't already been willing to believe almost anything about this town, I might have been shocked.

Oh, and the sheriff was there, too, of course.

The judge nodded to the sheriff and the sheriff nodded to the deputy and the deputy called out in a sonorous and unnecessarily loud voice, "All rise." We were all already standing except for the judge and the woman, and neither one of them stood at the command.

"Hear ye, hear ye, comes now the Honorable Jacob Borman of county court in the County of Lewis in the State of Nevada. All ye having business before this honorable court shall now present themselves."

The judge rapped twice with his gavel, and I suppose the court was officially in session after that. The amanuensis, a stringy woman with graying hair, wrinkles enough to make a prune jealous, and a severe, pinched, and prissy little mouth that would make a carp envious, began writing just as fast and furious as she could. I had no idea what all she could be scratching down at this point, but she was busy as all get-out regardless.

Sheriff Merlin stepped forward and said, "If it please the court, Your Honor, the state wishes to bring charges against one Robert Boyd, address unknown, on counts involving horse theft, breaking and entering, larceny, and public endangerment. You are, I believe, familiar with the background and facts in this matter."

Which was news to me. Other than the horse I still didn't know what Liam stole, although it seemed he'd broken in someplace in order to steal it. The public endangerment was a complete mystery to me.

"How does the defendant plead?" the judge asked. His voice was considerably more imposing than his appearance. And he did sound and act sober. I supposed that was something to be thankful for.

The deputy prodded me in the ribs and I took a half step forward in the halt and shuffling gait dictated by the ankle cuffs and short chain that restricted my movement. My hands were cuffed also, but this time in front again.

The deputy jabbed me in the kidney with the blunt and nasty end of a wooden baton. "Don't even think about it, mister."

"I'm not trying anything. I just want to talk to the judge and explain what's happened here. I just . . ."

The deputy jabbed me again. Harder this time.

"How d'you plead?" the sheriff growled. "That's all you say right now. Your chance to talk will come, but it isn't now. Just tell the judge how you plead, and we'll take you back upstairs."

"Not guilty," I called out loud and clear. "I didn't do anything. I—" The baton jabbed for a third time into the exact same already very sensitive spot. I shut my mouth, as I can be slow sometimes but not that slow.

My lower back hurt like hell.

"The prisoner will be bound over for trial, Sheriff, on the charges stated. Bond is set in the amount of twenty-five thousand dollars."

Twenty-five thousand. Uncle Edward could arrange that. Bond would at least get me out of jail so I could properly defend myself. And look for that damned Liam O'Day, too.

The judge rapped the bench with his gavel. "Is there further business before the court at this time, Sheriff?"

"No, Your Honor."

The judge whacked his bench again, and the deputy called, "All rise." We were all still standing, of course, except the judge and the amanuensis, and as before neither one of them paid any attention to the order.

The amanuensis finished whatever it was she'd been scribbling down, then sat up straighter from the hunched posture she'd been in and began gathering papers, ink, and pens together.

The judge stood—it was hard to tell while he was behind that broad, thronelike courtroom bench, but he didn't look to be much taller than Liam O'Day was—and yawned. "You'll be at the poker game tonight, John?"

"That I will, Jacob."

"Good. We missed taking your money while you were off chasing criminals."

"That'll be the day." I assumed the sheriff meant it was unlikely that the judge and whoever else constituted the "we" in that statement would take any of his money, not that he didn't chase criminals. And catch innocents while he was at it.

"Take him upstairs," the sheriff instructed the deputy, who grasped me by the arm and pushed, nearly unbalancing me because of my feet being shackled with such a short run of chain.

I'd had better days.

Chapter Seventeen

Being in a jail cell was a new, if unexciting, experience for me.

The cell had two walls of stone, as it was placed into a corner of the courthouse second story. The back and left side wall—leftward if one were standing in the corridor looking into the cell, that is—were made of mortared stone. The front and right side "walls" were formed of iron bars welded together in floor-to-ceiling verticals spaced about a handspan apart. Much too close together for even a child to pass through. Short horizontal pieces were welded in for reinforcement, these spaced roughly two feet apart one above another.

The door was made of the same grade of iron bar but with no key lock, as I might have expected had I ever in my life bothered to give thought to jail cells. Instead, there was a sliding track arrangement that ran along the ceiling of the cell area. A massive steel plate could be dragged back and forth along it by way of levers placed at the far end of the three-cell block of holding cells. This plate could be set to interfere with the opening of the door, thus effectively locking the door closed, or could be pulled back to allow the door to swing open. There was, therefore, no key to steal nor lock to pick, and nothing that could be reached from within the cell would have the slightest effect upon the secure containment of the prisoners.

It was an efficient system, and under other circumstances I might have admired it. One will understand, I hope, if I confess that I was not particularly enamored with it now.

I wanted *out* of there and quite honestly would have escaped if I'd had any opportunity to do so.

Within my cell were two flat, steel shelves that served as bunks. No mattresses were offered, but my bed was provided with a woolen blanket. One only. No pillow. No sheet. No comforts of any sort.

A galvanized metal bucket—without any lid—was provided for the, um, obvious purposes.

Of privacy there was none. Nor water. Nor softness. Nor hope.

There was a heavily barred window set into the back wall, but far from giving comfort it only mocked me by giving me sight of the freedoms to be found below.

From my window I could see a few of the streets and roofs of Lewisville. Could see people, some striding purposefully, other strolling at their leisure.

Heavy wagons rumbled back and forth along the street, as did buggies and light rigs. I saw very few saddle horses in use here.

Across the street and within my view were a general mercantile, a hardware, a small bank building, and a café. At times I smelled—or imagined I could smell—the sumptuous odors of breads baking and meats roasting.

That might have been wishful thinking though, for I was very hungry and there was virtually no air movement inside the cell. The window was unglazed but even so admitted no air, for there was no ventilation other than the windows in the three cells on this one side of the building. In winter I should think it would have been mercilessly frigid. Now, in spring, it remained agreeably removed from the outdoor heat courtesy of the foot-and-a-half-thick stone walls.

On the far side of the corridor outside the cells there was only a blank wall. I did not know what lay on the other side of the wall.

As for the two other cells, the middle one was much like my own save for having three walls of iron bars instead of my two. And the last cell down the line, the one closest to the heavy door leading out into the sheriff's office, was set up with four steel bunks arranged double-decker style, with two on either side of the floor area.

Each of the three measured roughly nine feet by seven, the nine representing the depth from front to back and seven being the approximate width, most of which was taken up by the two steel bunks with a narrow aisle in the exact center.

I was the sole prisoner in residence at the moment and did not know whether to regard that as a nuisance or a blessing. I would have liked to learn more about the people here. Especially I would have liked to know more about what Liam O'Day did to these people.

But facing anyone right then, even a stranger, would have been an embarrassment.

Perhaps it was just as well that I was left alone to make whatever adjustments I could.

My first order of business toward that end was to lie down on the unyielding steel of the bed and try to recoup strength through sleep.

Chapter Eighteen

Do not think that comfort or relaxation either one can be found by lying on the cold, hard surface of a steel plate. It cannot. What it does give you is the knowledge that one's body has lumps and protrusions on it that you've never suspected possessing. The steel finds every one of these and presses them into the relative softness of the body so that pain is developed behind each of them. Even after years of outdoor living with nothing but the ground for a bed—but padded with the comforts of a bedroll, I must confess—I was completely unprepared for the bed they gave me in the Lewis County Courthouse.

I hurt. I also slept, however, and that was greatly to the good, for I felt considerably better when I heard a door and footsteps. My guest proved to be the deputy I'd seen earlier for my arraignment. He was carrying a tray and a candle.

The tray contained a pewter bowl large enough to hold, I would judge, something more than a quart of material. The bowl was just small enough to fit through a horizontal opening in the bars of the cell door, the passageway set about waist high.

"Supper," the deputy announced.

"Thank you." I rose and met him at the door, where he slid the bowl through and then handed me a largish wooden spoon. "What," I asked, "is this?" The contents of the bowl were grayish white and lumpily granular with a glop of bright yellow butter melting in the middle.

"You never seen grits before?"

"Not if this is them, I haven't."

"Get used to 'em." He turned away and used the candle to light a sequence of oil lamps set along the corridor wall, well out of reach from the cells. Over his shoulder and without bothering to look at me he added, "I'll be back for the bowl an' spoon in ten, fifteen minutes."

"Don't I get something to drink?"

"Later." He went on with the chore of lighting the lamps, which had large reservoirs and reflectors to direct their light into the cells. The globes and reflectors were in need of cleaning, I noticed.

"I need to send a letter," I told him. "I want to arrange bail and hire a lawyer." I had long since realized that my impulse to protect the family from knowledge of my fate was not a sensible one. Had the posse conducted a lynching on the spot that charade would have been a mercy to my loved ones. Here in the county jail the idea was not nearly so attractive. I wanted out of here, and Uncle Edward could arrange that with a snap of his fingers, as he had both the wherewithal and the reputation to attract lawyers like flies to a cow pie if once the need of such services were known.

The deputy said nothing. He lighted the last of the five lamps on the wall, turned my way long enough to give me a skeptical and none-too-friendly glare, then disappeared back the way he'd just come.

I was left alone again, but this time with . . . supper. I gave the bowl a baleful look and, giving in to the inevitable, perched on the side of a bunk—the one with the blanket on it for sleeping and the other for sitting and, um, visiting? my choices of furniture were limited—to enjoy whatever this odd, porridgelike stuff was.

Chapter Nineteen

Grits are warm and filling. No flavor in them, understand, but they were served warm and in a quantity enough at least to let my stomach know it wasn't forgotten. More than that I would not claim for them, however.

Shortly after the pleasures of supper the deputy returned to collect the bowl and spoon. He carefully examined each before deciding that I hadn't stolen some part of either item, for what purpose I had no idea but he seemed to think there would be danger of me having . . . what? a wooden splinter to fight my way out? Oh well. I didn't really have to understand everything they did here. Just put up with it.

"May I have the letter-writing implements?" I asked.

His response was a noncommittal grunt. He left the cell area and returned moments later with a rubberized canvas water sack, which he hung by its thongs from the cell bars where I could get to it by reaching through them, and a tin cup that would fit between the bars.

"Thank you," I said. "I was asking about that letter so I can write to my family about a lawyer. I think . . ."

The deputy completed his task of tying the water bag in

place, handed me the tin cup, and without responding to my request left the cells again.

I could hear a very heavy and solid-sounding bar close in place on the outside of the door leading from the cells to the rest of the world.

I had a cup of water to wash down the gritty feeling left behind by the grits—well named, those—and went to stand idly at the window looking into the streets of Lewisville Flats. It was either that or try to sleep again, and if I napped any longer I would not be able to sleep that night.

I had had, it is true, better moments.

Chapter Twenty

There was a young woman, very pretty, with straw-blond hair that she wore piled high and not at all concealed under a jaunty little tea-saucer-sized cap. She carried a parasol but never opened it. Each morning she strolled up the street from the south and entered the bank building visible across the street from the courthouse. She remained inside the bank no more than a few minutes each day, then exited and went back the way she'd just come.

I never saw her more than that once each day, but she always did make that one appearance. In my fantasy I invested her with a make-believe life: She was the bank owner's beautiful daughter; her name was Imogene; robbers would attempt to hold up the bank while Imogene was present but I would thwart them, and Imogene would be forever grateful. Exactly how I was to accomplish this from the inside of a jail cell I did not bother to work out.

In any event, Imogene—or whatever her name really was—was but one of the ordinary and routine sights of Lewisville Flats that I came to know by way of my window. There was the milk deliveryman who abused the pair of undernourished little burros that pulled his wagon. A young man with curly hair who rode a stunningly handsome black gelding with a coat so slick and glossy it looked like oil would drip onto the ground from it. The town barber who was bald. Businessmen of varying sizes, ages and shapes who regularly appeared at the bank or the café or both. I came, if not to know them, at least then to observe and recognize them.

The lamps in the café were burning well before dawn, presumably when the baking was started, and the doors were opened soon afterward. The café did a brisk business from just before daybreak almost until time for the midday meal and was overflowing with customers until past noon. Then the doors were closed, a blind drawn, and that was that for the day. There must have been a back-alley entry, because I never saw the owner or helpers other than a rare glimpse of blindingly white apron when the place was being opened for business or shut for the day.

The town also had what seemed to me a disproportionately large number of very heavy wagons on its streets. And from somewhere off in the distance there was at all times the steady *thump-thump-thump* of extraordinarily heavy pounding going on day and night, so constant it seemed a mutual heartbeat of the community, ever present and eventually unnoticed in its regularity.

I eventually concluded, on the basis of things I'd read even though I had never personally heard such a thing before, that Lewisville Flats must support a mine of some nature and that this pounding must be the sound made by a stamp mill busy breaking mineral ores for processing into . . . whatever.

Oh, the things one can observe and learn and imagine when one has nothing more interesting to do than to stand in a second-floor window and look out upon the town of strangers.

I had days upon days of this dubious pleasure. Five, six, the number began to be unclear to me, for one day was the same as the one before and the nights a lonely and miserable exercise in sleepless discomfort and worry.

I was given two meals a day. Usually grits but sometimes fried potatoes. Once, presumably on Sunday, there was bacon and hard rolls for breakfast and rice with brown gravy for supper.

The deputy never spoke no matter how often I implored him to bring me writing materials, and the sheriff made no appearances inside the cell area.

The discomforts of incarceration, I was learning, lay in the isolation rather than in any external or physical threat.

Of course, that observation would be subject to change if hanging became again an issue.

Chapter Twenty-one

"Help! Help! They won't let me see a lawyer. Help! Help! I need a lawyer."

I stood at the window. I shouted. Loudly. Over and over and over again. After all, if that mule-headed deputy wouldn't listen to me . . .

It took, I would estimate, perhaps two hours for my very public braying to bring results. I heard the cell door open— with a slam and a bang this time—and lo and behold, the sheriff himself came into the corridor with his deputy close on his heels.

Actually, by that time I was more than a little pleased to receive some reward for my efforts, because I wouldn't have been able to keep it up much longer. My voice was by then becoming hoarse, and my throat hurt.

"Good afternoon, Sheriff," I said, taking care to be calm and polite. I meekly turned away from the window and met my guests at the front bars of the cell.

The sheriff gave me a suspicious look and then gave his deputy another. "What the hell is going on here, Ron?"

The deputy, whose name I only now heard, shrugged.

"I've been asking daily to see you, sir," I put in. "I need to hire a lawyer. That is to say, my family will want to provide me with a lawyer. I need writing materials so I can notify them."

The sheriff looked at Ron. "Is he telling the truth?"

"Sure. But John, you haven't heard the rest of the stuff he's been ranting at me."

"What do you mean, Ron?"

The deputy inclined his head in my direction. "Go ahead, big boy. Tell the sheriff here who your family are an' how you expect them to bail you out twenty-five thousand dollars' worth."

"It's true, Sheriff. I do expect my family to post surety bond for me."

"You do, eh?"

"Yes, sir."

"Your folks got that kind of money, do they, Bob?" For a moment I kind of forgot that it was me he was speaking to, the sheriff thinking me to be Bob Boyd rather than Boyd Little.

"Yes, sir, they do. You probably have heard of them. My true name is Boyd Little. My uncle is Edward Little of the Bar X Bar ranch."

The sheriff snorted. "So you're one of the Littles, you say."

"Yes, sir, that's right."

"Robert Boyd is just an alias you use for your crimes, is that it?"

"No, sir, I've committed no crimes. Not here, not anywhere. Robert Boyd is . . . Do we really want to go into all of this? The point is, my family is well able to arrange my bond and a suitable lawyer to defend me. I need writing materials so I can contact them, and your deputy here has been very unpleasant to me. He consistently ignores my requests for pen and paper. I've been asking every day to see you, but he won't even answer me. Believe me, Sheriff, my uncle and the rest of my family are going to be *very* upset with you when they learn about all this."

"Ed Little, you say."

61

"Yes, sir."

"Of the Bar X Bar."

"Yes, sir."

"Your shouting accomplished one thing, Bob. It brought me in here so we can talk."

"Yes, sir. I'm sorry about that. I don't mean to cause a public disturbance, but I couldn't think of anything else that might get your attention."

"Uh-huh. Well, let me tell you something, Bob. Any more of that and I'll consider it to be a public nuisance. I'll come into that cell with a dozen men if that's what it takes, and we will chain you away from the window and put a gag in your mouth so you can't shout anymore. Do you understand me?"

"Yes, sir, I do. I'll not shout again. I only wanted to let you know about my true name and the writing materials that I need."

The sheriff looked at Ron. "If he gives you any more trouble, you let me know. You don't have to put up with the likes of Mr. Boyd here."

"Little," I corrected him.

The sheriff gave me a dirty look. "I wasn't talking to you, was I."

"Sorry, sir."

He looked at the deputy again. "And do not under any circumstances allow this lunatic to bother decent people. That would include the Littles." He sighed and shook his head sadly. "Having that much money . . . it just makes you a target for all the grifters and liars and beggars in the country, I suppose. And just imagine it. A juicer like him claiming to be one of the family. I feel sorry for them, Ron. I really do."

The two of them, sheriff and deputy, left me alone to stew in some very uncomfortable juice. Having nothing to do with juicers. Whatever *those* were.

Chapter Twenty-two

Despair is a most ugly thing. I felt the weight of it crushing down upon me day and night and daytime again.

I was locked up for a crime I hadn't committed and about which I knew nothing. And for this crime I faced the threat of hanging. The thought of that . . . I found it difficult to swallow as the lump in my throat expanded so that I could hardly breathe, and there was a tingling of the skin where a hangman's noose might press.

What would it feel like to walk out into the very courtyard that I could see from my cell window? To walk on trembling legs into sunshine for the last time in a life too short? To climb the thirteen steps and hear the hollow thump of boot heels on pine planks? To have to stand there trussed like a goose for the roasting pan, arms and legs contained by thick leather straps while some cruel stranger put a hood over the top of my head and draped it to my shoulders?

It would be hot beneath the black cloth, I thought. I could as good as smell the sun-warmed linen already, there in my cell. It would be hot and there would be men on either side of me taking rough hold of my arms lest I faint and slump down before the trap opened that would drop me all the way to eternity.

The only senses still available to me would be scent and hearing. The sheriff would read aloud the court's judgment. Crowds of people who never knew me and never would, would taunt and shout from around the gallows scaffold. The hangman would place the noose.

Would it be heavy, that noose with the thirteen twists? Would it be tight? It would have to be tight, I supposed. He would want the knot to lie in its proper place, and so I suppose it would have to be snug. Not yet hanged and already cutting off the ability to breathe.

There in my cell I gulped in great quantities of air, now while I still could. My legs felt weak, and I hurriedly sat on the side of the spare bunk that I'd come to think of as my settee. My chest heaved, and I felt light in the head and somewhat dizzy as my breathing became more a doglike panting than normal breath, quick and shallow and breathing out very little, although anxious to draw more air into overburdened lungs.

I lay back onto the hard, cold steel of the jail cell bunk and imagined the feel of being there on the gallows. The heat. The shouting crowd. The rope. Oh, God! The rope.

And then the drop. I hated to fall. Perhaps because I am so large of body and hit with such force, I hate to fall. I fell from a tree once when I was a small boy and I've hated it ever since. Hate even to fall from the back of a horse. That fear, told to no one ever, has oddly made me a better rider than I might otherwise have been, for it has taught me to be unusually difficult to dislodge from the saddle lest I fall again.

My cousins and the cowhands back home have sometimes marveled at how tenaciously I will cling to the back of even the wildest mount. I never participate in their impromptu bucking contests, and so they create their own fun with me sometimes. I've learned to be very careful to inspect my saddle and cinches for burrs or other annoyances that they will sometimes employ to create an amusement for themselves.

But to fall from the gallows . . . to feel the earth drop out from beneath one's feet and then to drop. To the end of the hangman's rope. Until . . .

I will confess that I was weak and trembling and sick to my stomach at the imagined thoughts of it all, and if a few tears leaked from the corners of my eyes, well, who was to care with all my dear ones so far away and never knowing of my awful plight.

I lay there feeling thoroughly miserable, quite thoroughly sorry for myself. Down at the far end of the cell area I heard the thump of the door opening—would the sound of the trapdoor have that same dull, heavy quality? I wondered—and loud voices. They were bringing in a drunk, I supposed, or some petty offender.

Those came and went, but they were two cells distant, and I never had any commerce with them. Drunks have always disgusted me anyway, and in my mood of self-pity I held no interest in any of them. I ignored their taunts—the crowd gathered for my hanging would probably sound much the same except on a far larger scale—and their few questions or comments and tried to convince myself that these people did not exist.

In my mind, whenever I could, I much preferred to take myself back to the north of Nevada. Onto the ranges and mountains, the seemingly barren but oh so lovely grazing lands and the jewel-like hidden pockets where water and lush grasses could be found—I knew each of those from boyhood—and the high crags where eagles flew and the wind came sweet and deep into a man's lungs.

And so I ignored these philistines around me and took fancied excursions homeward.

And sometimes . . . sometimes I cried.

Chapter Twenty-three

Morning. Another Sunday, I was guessing. I tried to keep track of the days but could not, for distractions intruded. And I didn't really have any starting point to go by, anyway. I was only assuming that it was on Sundays when I received a bit of meat in my meals.

Another clue was that Saturday was when all the drunks were brought in, and last night had been a busy one. The deputy and his rarely seen helpers must have dragged in eight or ten of them the previous night. The drunks sang and puked and lay noisily about the cell at the far end until they became a true annoyance, but I knew better than to so much as acknowledge them. The townspeople were already anticipating an early hanging, as some of the other common-cell visitors had informed me, and the comments I received from that end of the cells could be crude and irritating. Best not to allow anything to start if I could at all help it.

So on this morning I lay as usual with my back to that far cell, pretending to sleep when the deputy came in to fetch his now sober overnight guests out to where they could be warned or fined or whatever it was they did with them.

"You. You. Now you," I heard him. "Yes, you. Come on now, damn you." The words were followed by a rather solidly meaty sound and a series of yelps and scrapes that I did not recognize. Then: "You hit me, you little son of a bitch, you hit me."

There was another of those odd noises, and the deputy angrily shouted, "That does it, buster. I'm charging you so you just stay right there. You ain't going anywhere this morning."

The pugnacious fellow who'd just thrown away his opportunity to walk free—something I could not imagine a sane person doing—made a crude suggestion, but he apparently stopped scuffling with the deputy, for I heard no more actual conflict afterward.

The cell door rolled open and shut several times before all the drunks were released and disposed of downstairs so that I was more or less alone in the cells once again.

There was no longer any point in pretending to be asleep, for they would be bringing breakfast soon and I was hungry.

I pushed the blanket aside and stood, yawning and stretching.

Out of some small curiosity I glanced down the way toward the large cell at the end.

The prisoner there stood at the cell bars. Facing me. Grinning hugely.

"You son of a bitch!" I roared.

Chapter Twenty-four

"Boyd. Laddy. It's missin' me that you've been, innit?"

"Liam, you miserable little son—"

"Na, na, lad. Calm ye'self. There's a wee mistake been made, but nothin' we can't put right b'tween us."

"Damn right there's a mistake been made, and now you'll pay for it. They want to *hang* me. Did they tell you that? Hanging. Me. For something *you* did. What was it you did, anyway? No, never mind that. I don't even care what you did. Just so long as you're the one who hangs for it and not me." I turned to the window, intent on resuming my bellowing so the sheriff would be brought. Furious, of course. But he'd be brought. I could be reasonably sure of that after the last time, even though his presence would only be intended to inflict punishment for this continued transgression.

"Don't be botherin' the lads at their worship na, Boyd me boyo. It's you I've come here t' save, is it not?"

"Save? You expect me to believe a thing like that, you low and miserable little wisp of scum? You get yourself thrown into jail and wind up next to me so—"

"Think, lad. Why would I bring meself back t' a miserable hole like this save for the chanct t' see justice done? I'm here for you, lad. Here t' lead you t' the freedom ye desarve. Which ye richly do, lad. But let's do this in a sensible manner, shall we? If ye tell the coppers all ye know, ye'll only be implicatin' the both of us. Think, Boyd. Ye have the power t' put me inta that cell with ye, but never will ye convince yon yokels that ye weren't my partner in crime at the very least of it.

"Squawk like ye want an' ye're only settin' rope 'round my neck beside yours. Ye wouldn't take naught from off yer own neck. An' where, I ask ye, is the profit in that? Trust me, boyo Boyd, an' I'll have us both breathin' deep as free men ought."

He continued to grin.

"Trust me."

Trust Liam O'Day. Oh, to be sure. Once I'd trusted him. Now I faced hanging. For *his* crimes.

Of course I would trust him.

In a pig's eye, I would trust him.

"Trust me," the grinning little leprechaun crooned soft and cheery. "Trust in me."

I'd trust him. Damn right I would. But first let me get my hands around that scrawny little throat.

"Trust me, boyo."

Chapter Twenty-five

"Say na, sure an' it's a apology I'd be owin' ye. Came outa a fearsome dream, don't ye see, an' I thought 'twas you as was hurtin' me. Except 'twas only a dream, y'see, and I'd be ever grateful if ye find it in yer heart t' forgive me. Not that I expect ye t' drop the charges. No indeed, yer worship. I deserve the full penalty o' the law there. 'Deed I do, yer worship."

I could see that Ron was impressed by the wide-eyed sincerity of the little man's apology. So much so that the deputy actually spoke to him. "Apology accepted," he grunted. "And I expect I can forgive you. I haven't written out any charges. Reckon I don't have to. Have your breakfast. It's already here, so you might as well eat it. Then I'll let you out when I come back for the plates."

"Thankee, yer worship, thankee." Liam practically groveled. Grinning all the while.

Was Ron impressed? More than a little. I observed him pluck something off the plate that was intended for me and drop it onto Liam's before he handed that one through the open slot. I suspected it was the reverent way Liam said "your worship" that so charmed the deputy.

"I'll be back in a half hour or so."

"Thankee, yer worship. Ye're too kind."

The deputy wordlessly came down to my end of the corridor and shoved my tin plate through the bars. I had to grab it quick to keep it from falling, for he just pushed it through and then let go. If I hadn't hurried to take hold of it the plate and contents alike would have wound up on the filth of the jail cell floor.

The Sunday-morning breakfast consisted of biscuits and bacon, a veritable feast compared with grits and water.

The biscuits were heavy things, soggy and doughy and not quite thoroughly cooked. Which was just as well. Being leaden and lumpy things, they would fill the stomach and stay with a man for hours. Besides, they kind of reminded me of my own cooking when I was riding out away from home and had to make do without my mother's light-as-feathers biscuits.

"How many slabs of bacon do you have there?" I asked once the door at the end of the corridor was shut and Ron was safely out of hearing.

"Five. You?"

"Three." Dammit. It was one of my pieces of bacon Ron added to Liam's plate.

"Here, laddy. I've no hunger any the way. I'll take this wee lump of . . ." He eyed a biscuit critically, then grinned again and shrugged. "I'll just be keepin' whate'er this thing be an' pass along the rest."

"But that's your breakfast," I protested.

"Nonsense, boyo. B'sides. I can be buyin' myself a proper meal quick as I'm sprung from this lovely place. You canna say the same."

"What are you going to do? Throw the stuff across to me?" We were separated by the middle cell.

"No need, laddy. Trust me."

I rolled my eyes. We'd had a talk already. A "wee chat," as Liam put it. And I'd come to accept the reality that putting Liam into jail with me would not be much of an accomplishment. Instead, I'd accepted his solemn promise that as soon as he was released he would contact my family

71

an appeal that they come to my rescue with bond
and a squadron of square-rigged lawyers under full

But . . . trust him? I was hard-pressed to do so. Had no
choice, of course. But even so . . .

Liam knelt beside the bars between the large cell where
he was and the middle cell. He tipped the plate and dumped
its contents onto his forearm for safekeeping, then tilted the
plate so that he could slide it between the bars and set it
down on the floor inside the middle cell. He reached
through again to deposit the bacon and biscuits back onto
the plate, save for one biscuit that he held back for himself.

Then, first sliding the tin plate back and forth a few times,
presumably to get a feel for its weight, he gave the plate a
mighty push, sending it skittering across the cell floor and
beneath the steel cots to end up against the bars on my side
of the floor.

"Help ye'sel'," he cheerfully said, "an' be so good as t'
pass the platter back when ye're done, laddy."

I had the impression that this knowledge of trafficking
between cells was not a newly acquired skill for little Mr.
O'Day.

Not that I was complaining.

I hastened to transfer bacon and biscuits from his plate
to mine and then reached through the bars with the intent
to return the now-empty plate to him.

"Careful, lad," he told me. "Too little, see, an' it doesn't
get here. Too much an' it c'n bound back out o' my reach.
Just enou' is what's needed."

I frowned. Skittered the plate back and forth a few
times—as Liam had done moments earlier—to get the feel
of it, then gave the plate a shove.

It amazed me to discover the sense of satisfaction I received when the plate slid breezily across the floor and con-
tacted the bars on the far side with but a light and harmless
tap.

"Lovely," Liam cooed. "Ye're a natural jailbird if e'er I
saw one, Boyd me boyo."

I suppose that was intended to be a compliment. Of a sort.

Still and all, I was now well blessed with bacon and biscuit and could sit down to the first truly filling meal I'd enjoyed since . . . well, since back when I was still a free man.

That long ago.

Chapter Twenty-six

For me Ron had nothing but grunts and scowls. With Liam, who just an hour or so earlier had tried to deck him, the deputy was as windy as a fresh breeze. He chattered away like they were old friends when he returned to crank the cell door open so he could release the little man.

He let Liam out into the corridor, then paused to send a glare in my direction. "You," he snarled.

I looked at him. Didn't much feel like speaking, though.

"I'm gonna set a mop and bucket inside this door, then open your cell too. While I'm gone you can clean this mess. And mind you do it right or there'll be no supper for you."

Ron's attention was fixed on me, but slightly to his rear Liam sort of raised up onto his tiptoes and lifted his arms.

"The sheriff is just outside this door," Ron said. And Liam settled back onto his heels. Whatever he'd had in mind was abandoned at that news. "If you try anything he'll shoot you, and I'd hate to see the hangman cheated out of his pay."

I still didn't feel like saying a damn thing. Not hardly.

Ron let Liam loose in the outer office and stood in the

doorway long enough to drag the mop and bucket inside. Then he hauled the heavy door shut behind him and once again I heard the solid thump of a heavy bar being put in place.

I was alone again. But with a full belly and more freedom of motion than I'd known since that posse arrested me.

More important than either of those things, though, was that now I had an ally—of sorts, anyhow—on the outside.

Liam had promised he would contact my family about bail and a lawyer.

For the first time in quite some while I once again had hope.

Chapter Twenty-seven

"All right, you. You're going to get your comeuppance now." The deputy gave me a smug look as he passed my bowl of gruel—all right, grits . . . but I was coming to think of it as gruel—through the opening in the bars. "Your trial is set for Friday. With luck you'll hang Saturday morning."

"That can't be right. I haven't even seen a lawyer yet. Who's going to defend me? Who will . . ."

The deputy wasn't listening. He turned and walked away without another word.

I was . . . devastated is not nearly strong enough a term. Shattered. Crushed. Pick any description you care to name and it still wouldn't be anything close to the truth. This was . . . what? . . . Tuesday. Or Wednesday. Tuesday, I thought.

The trial would be on Friday, he'd said. The hanging—oh Lord!—on Saturday. Liam got out of his deliberate overnight lockup—he'd said he started a ruckus so he could get himself thrown into jail where he could see me, just as he'd deliberately punched Ron that morning so he would not be released along with the others—on Sunday morning.

Even if he wrote the letter to my family immediately it

would not leave the post office until Monday. It would take—what?—a week at least to travel from Lewisville Flats to our postal box in Kyne Springs.

And once the letter arrived there it would have to sit in the pigeonhole until the next Saturday when someone from the Bar X Bar might reasonably be expected to show up and claim the week's mail. It was exceptionally rare for any of us to have any need for town services in the middle of the week, and Saturdays were the normal shopping days, as it took the full day to drive down to town, load the wagon with whatever was needed, and return. Even starting out before dawn, it would be late at night before whoever made the journey got home again.

And sometimes—please no—sometimes whoever was assigned the shopping chore did not remember to pick up the mail that week. After all, mail was a rarity. Most times our box would remain empty for weeks on end, and the only time we were enthused about the prospect of picking it up was when a new catalog was expected or someone had ordered something that was due to arrive soon.

Good Lord, it could be three weeks before Liam's letter would even arrive at the ranch. How much longer before Uncle Edward would select a suitable lawyer? Then still more time for the lawyer to stir himself to make the journey down here.

A month should be the *least* amount of time necessary for me to see the lawyer. Perhaps more time for a draft to clear the local bank so that I could be released on bail. Or if cash was sent, then time would be required for Uncle Edward to collect it from his accounts and entrust it to the lawyer.

If he did trust a lawyer with money. More likely, Uncle Edward would send one of the cousins down to bail me out of jail.

And what a humiliating thought that one was.

I could just see the smirking, suspicious, superior look Jared would give me. Or George or Eddie the Second, who we all called Deuce because he hated the nickname so. Except Uncle Edward would never trust Deuce with a job like that. Jared, probably. Now that I myself was out of the mix. After all, I was the one trusted to take Uncle Edward's cash south to buy our horses. And hadn't I made a thorough mess of *that* responsibility?

I'd never be able to hold my head up among the cousins, not ever again.

But then, better to go home shamed, I suppose, than to die at the end of an undeserved hangman's rope down here among strangers.

Oh Lord! Saturday. The deputy said I might die as soon as this coming Saturday.

I set the bowl of grits aside untouched. For the first time since I came down with an epizootic at age eleven, I had no appetite whatsoever.

Chapter Twenty-eight

Day turned into night and night into day again and I scarcely knew the difference. I sat where I was in a state of deep despair, dimly aware but not at all caring when someone came into the corridor and left again. The deputy, probably, carrying bowls of grits or oat porridge. I didn't look to see. Didn't care anyway who it was or what his purpose. It was not a lawyer come to save me from the gallows, and that was all I cared or could think about.

Tuesday passed in that fashion and so did Wednesday, although by Wednesday evening my belly was commencing to complain about the treatment I was giving it. I ignored those rumblings just as I ignored the sheriff when he came and tried to capture my attention.

That man had done more than enough evil to me already. I didn't need his lectures on top of everything else.

As for the trial . . . my cause was hopeless and therefore I held no hope within me. None.

If they intended to try me—for crimes that I still never had described to me and of which I was ignorant as well as innocent—there was no point even in attempting to represent myself.

The people here had their minds firmly made up on the subject of Boyd Little. Or Robert Boyd, as they insisted I was. That part was my own fault, of course.

But what a horrid shock this whole thing would be to my mother. I was her baby and she loved me. To know that I'd died by public hanging, a convicted and condemned criminal, would burden her for all her days.

It would be a mercy, I thought, if Liam's letter never reached them.

Had I the capacity to do so, I would have called that missive back so that it never would be delivered. So the family would never learn of my fate. Better they know none of it than for them to attempt a rescue only to find their efforts too late.

They would have my body disinterred and taken home for burial on the hillside where our family cemetery was. My mother would weep and my father quietly grieve.

Better if I could simply disappear and they assume I'd died at the hands of a bandit than for all of this to take place.

I wished now that I hadn't asked Liam to write to them. I wished . . .

"Psst! Boyd me boyo."

I looked about, but there was no one there in the cells to see.

The deputy must have come in unnoticed to offer me supper, for the lamps in the corridor brightly burned and the water bag bulged now where before it had been flat and nearly empty.

But there was no one in the corridor or in either of the other cells.

I was alone. Completely, hopelessly alone in my cell.

"Boyd, lad. Over here."

The voice seemed to come from the window. An impossibility, of course. The block of cells was on the second floor of the courthouse, and there were no stairs anywhere on this side of the building. God knew I'd spent enough time peering out of that window. I knew for a fact what was out there and what was not.

"Come here, old son. I've a wee giftie for ye."

I'd gone daft. Completely out of my senses. The strain of it all, I supposed. I wanted so badly to call Liam's letter back that I was imagining I could hear the little man's voice.

That had to be the explanation.

"Dammit, Boyd, I can see ye settin' there on yer fat arse. Now stand up, lad, an' coom t' this'ere portal."

It was an awfully powerful hallucination. I had to give it that. I would almost have sworn . . .

I saw a hand poke through the bars.

"Liam?"

"Not so loud, dammit. Now c'mere, will you?"

Incredible. And yet . . .

I stood. Went as directed to the window, where the grinning—did the miserable little leprechaun *ever* look glum? I rather ungratefully wondered—fellow was somehow clinging to the bars. How he had gotten there I could not begin to understand. But there he was. He had . . . ah, that explained it. He had a harness sort of contraption made of ropes that hung from the roof and held him in place outside my window.

And he had another coil of rope draped over his shoulders. Two of them, as it turned out, for he quickly slipped one coil over his head and pushed it through the bars and into my hands.

"Tie one end t' the leg o' yon bunk, laddy."

"Why?"

"No time t' be long winded, old son. Just do as I say. Ye'll see the need in a few minutes, I promise."

I frowned and stood there stupid and mute while Liam took the other coil from his shoulder and tied one end through the bars, weaving it back and forth several times and affixing it in a quick but careful design before he tied it off and dropped the rest of that coil to the earth.

I began to comprehend at last.

"Liam, you can't—"

"Hush, boyo. I can, an' so can you. Now do as I tell ye. I'll have this out quick as Nellie York sheds 'er knickers. Quick now, Boyd. Quickly."

And he was gone. Dropped—more like he slid, really, though I didn't see how he did it nor understand it—away from the window and down the side of the stonework courthouse wall.

I was left standing there with nothing but the dark of night to look at.

Still feeling a trifle dazed from coming out of the stupor I'd been in, I looked rather blankly at the coil of rope I was holding—at least that was proof enough that I was not imagining this entire event, for the rope was real and it was in my hands to see and touch and smell of it if I wished—then after several seconds made a valiant attempt to recover my wits.

I went over to the foot of my bed, knelt, and tied one end of the rope there as Liam had said I should.

Chapter Twenty-nine

The rope Liam tied onto the cell bars came taut under some great strain, and, curious, I went over to the window to look out.

It was dark and I could see little, especially since there was light inside the cell block and none outside. Even so, I could tell that there was movement of some sort on the ground out in the parklike square that lay between the courthouse and the street.

I could hear the jangle of chain and the sharp, delicate snap of a whip. Soon after that I heard the pop of big hoofs beating the earth as a team of mighty horses laid hard into their collars.

Comprehending at last what was afoot here, I jumped back away from the window. If the rope parted, I could get a ragged end of it in the face.

The rope, thank goodness, held and with a high-pitched shriek of groaning protest the entire window frame was jerked loose from the stone surrounding.

Frame, bars, everything disappeared, whisked away by the enormous strength of those horses on the ground below.

Frank Roderus

I can be slow sometimes, but I am not completely stupid.

I grabbed hold of the rope Liam had given me, tugged once on it to make sure my knot would hold, then shoved my overlarge body into the gaping hole where those bars so recently were.

Chapter Thirty

"C'mon, boyo. Hurry now."

The admonition was unnecessary. Before I had time to respond, my left hand slipped and I had to turn loose of the rope or suffer a serious burn on my right, and that is something that no cowhand willingly accepts. I fell the last six or so feet. Probably, I later reflected, the same approximate distance that the hangman's drop would have given me.

I hit, tumbled, rolled when I fell, handling it as if coming off a rank horse, and so was able to avoid serious damage.

Liam was already at my side. He grabbed me by the arm and hustled me across the grass toward the wagon.

"Mount, lad. We've ridin' t' do this night, an' quick about it lest we both hang for felons."

My own good bay was there carrying—a wild surge of joy leapt through me, let me tell you—carrying my own good saddle on his back. Beside the bay was another horse at least as tall but much lighter boned. I could not tell much about this one in the dark. It was to this animal that Liam raced, clambering into the saddle like a squirrel scampering up a tree while I stepped with immeasurable relief onto the bay.

"Stay wi' me now, boyo." Liam leaned down from his perch atop the dark and leggy horse and snatched up the driving lines of the wagon team. I did not understand why for a moment. Then I realized that he intended creating confusion for the posse that was certain to give chase. Again.

Now that we were no longer afoot, Liam abandoned silence in favor of a whoop of delight and a dig of his heels into the tall horse's flank. Dragging the wagon team with him, he careened out into the street, swung away to the north, and brought them all into a dead run toward the horizon.

I was with them every wild and exhilarating jump of it.

I was free. For however long or short a time, I now tasted freedom once more.

Hallelujah!

Chapter Thirty-one

A man feels a sense of freedom anytime he is on horseback. A mounted man feels himself to be the master of his own fate. I'd known that since boyhood. Now I was learning that this feeling is intensified a thousandfold when his ride is an escape from death itself.

I was giddy with it. Dizzy. As if drunk on hard spirits.

And I loved it.

Remorse to be defying the law? Not a wisp of it. I was free and the gallows were behind and if I never saw nor heard of Lewisville Flats again that would suit me fine.

We rode hard and as fast as the wagon team could run, making an awful racket as the traces jangled and the wagon thumped and bumped and rattled.

Liam let out another whoop as we left the outskirts of town behind, and I roared out another even louder and gayer than his.

The air itself tasted crisp and clean and effervescent, and the pounding of hoofs on the road was music as fine as any composer ever devised.

I leaned forward in my saddle and let out a "ki-yi-yi" as

the wind rushed past my ears and ruffled my hair.

God, it felt fine.

I felt alive, deeply and truly alive. And keenly aware of it.

That was the thing. All too many pleasures are discovered only in retrospect. Not this mad, bubbling exhilaration. It filled and delighted me, and I could joyously have ridden at breakneck pace until the end of time. It was all I could do to bring myself to hold the bay at a pace to match that of the wagon team. I wanted to ride full out and belly down to the ends of the earth and devil take the hindmost.

"Yee haw, Liam. Ride on!"

Chapter Thirty-two

"Hold up, Liam. We got to stop."

It was coming daybreak and we'd been on the move throughout the night. We'd stayed with the wagon a good two hours, the platter-sized hoofs of the draft horses and the broad iron tires on the wheels churning the ground to cover our tracks. With luck the posse wouldn't even know that we had the saddle horses.

And if they did know they would have a terrible time trying to work out where we'd left the road. Liam had scouted the ground ahead of the escape—this time; apparently he hadn't done such a proper job of planning after he did whatever it was that landed me in jail—so we turned off the road at a place where the ground consisted of great sheets of native stone and no hoofprints would be left for— what was his name again? ah, yes, Dan; that one—for the tracker to follow. Damn him and his meanness, anyway.

We'd left the road and the team there, lashing the tiring team so they were still going at a run when we veered away from them. Then we'd headed east into some rough and very empty country.

89

Now it was morning and the horses were weary. For that matter, so was I. That mad rush of excitement had dwindled sometime during the night and was replaced with worry.

I was free, yes, but I was also by now a wanted man. An outlaw! It was something I scarcely believed my own self, and the family would never understand how this came to be.

"Stop, Liam."

"We can'na . . ."

"It isn't for us. The horses need a breather. Now stop. We'll get down and walk for a while. That's right. And loosen your horse's cinches. That's it. Let them dangle so the horse can breathe easier. Did you think to bring any water?"

"A wee container only, lad. There's na enou' fer the creatures."

"If there's not enough, Liam, then it's not enough for us. Not them. Whatever there is, they get first."

"But—"

"Liam, you killed the last horse you tried to run away on. So while I will freely defer to your judgment when it comes to jails and jail breaks, I think you should listen to me when the subject is getting miles out of your horse."

"Och! But dinna make me look while ye pour out the last o' our water."

"We'll replace it soon enough. There's water right over there a piece." I pointed.

"What, lad. Ye be knowin' this land?"

"No, but I have eyes, don't I? It's daybreak. Have you been paying attention to the whitewings? They fly to water first thing. You just watch the direction they take and follow it. There will be water somewhere on that line."

"Be damned," Liam exclaimed.

"Yes, you probably will be," I agreed as I fished inside the saddlebags—whose I did not know—that were tied onto my saddle. "Do you have a bandanna?" I could see plainly enough that he did. A gaudy red one as yet unfaded by sun or washing was tied at his throat. Its color clashed rather badly with the red of his hair. And, for that matter, of his complexion.

"Aye."

"May I borrow it, please?"

"Ye'll not be blowin' that great ugly nose o' yours in my new—"

"I need it to take care of the horses."

"Oh." He untied the article in question and gave it to me. I crumpled it into a wad and poured water on it, then used the sopping wet cloth to sponge out the nostrils of both horses. It would refresh them almost as well as a proper drink.

Liam's expression fell when he saw what I was doing and his nose wrinkled with disgust when I returned the now filthy and snot-crusted bandanna to him. "Eeiou!"

"Don't be such a sissy. If you don't want to wear it, give it to me. The moisture will feel good on your neck."

He made a face. But he did put the bandanna back around his neck. He didn't admit it, but I could tell from looking at him that he liked the feel of the cool cloth on hot, dry skin.

I took up the reins of my bay. "Follow me. We'll fill our bellies with water before long."

Chapter Thirty-three

We held to a generally north-by-northeast route throughout
that day and stopped for the night along the east side of a
sharp, knifelike ridge that turned into a small mountain a
little farther to the north.

The flats off to the east were barren and sunbaked and
not good for raising much except maybe lizards and rattle-
snakes.

I'd found us a dandy spot to stop, though, where a seep
of sweet water trickled out of the rocks and down onto the
ground, where it quickly disappeared into the sand. What I
did was to scoop out a hollow and stick Liam's hat into it
for the water to collect. I had to use Liam's hat for the job,
because mine had gotten lost sometime over the past couple
weeks and I was bareheaded despite the burn of the sun.
That was an annoyance, but not so much of a one as a noose
would've been.

Anyway, the water dribbling into the hat collected fast
enough that every fifteen or twenty minutes we had enough
to give to one of the horses and then to fill our own bellies.

"Sit down, Liam," I suggested along about the time the

sun disappeared and we could be pretty certain there would be no posse coming at us, at least not right away.

"Aye, laddie, 'tis time we sing some o' the sweet songs o' our youth."

"In a minute," I told him. "First there's a couple things I want to ask you."

"Aye, boyo. Anything."

"Liam, what did you *do* back there to get those folks so mad at you? Or more to the point, to get them so mad at *me*, thinking it was me that did whatever it was."

He grinned and laughed just a little. "I've a talent, Boyd me auld son. An' a fine talent it 'tis."

"And that would be?"

"Juice, lad. I'm an artist with the juice, if I do say so. Learnt the craft in the mines over Colorado way, an' if I do say so . . . as 'deed I do . . . there's none better."

"Juice," I repeated. "And what, may I ask, is juice?"

Liam's grin became all the larger. "Nitro, boyo. Nitroglycerin. I c'n peel mineral-bearin' ore off a stope wall slick as the Widow Mabry peels an apple. Except in this case, y'see, it was a safe door that I peeled loose, my talents not bein' properly utilized nor appreciated by certain folk back in that cursed town."

"You robbed a safe," I said. "Is that it?"

"Aye, son. Up t' the roof. Down inta the bank. Boom goes the door. An' out goes I. Nothin' to it."

"And the horse, Liam? If I remember correctly there was something about horse theft."

"Well, I dinna ha' one o' me own, did I? An' I had t' get away on somethin'. So I took the minin' engineer's horse, damn 'is eyes."

I assumed he meant the engineer, not the horse, with that indication of displeasure.

I looked out toward the hobbled black animal that Liam was riding now. I raised my eyebrows, and Liam grinned again.

"Personal mount o' the gentle man as owns the town's two finest gamin' establishments an' three o' the sportin' houses. Much better taste 'e has than that SOB o' a engineer too, I'm tellin' you."

I had to agree. The black was splendid. I sighed. "Liam, what we have to do now is simple. I've been thinking long and hard about it today, and what I think we have to do is this. We'll head straight north from here. Just ride on north until we hit the railroad and then follow it west to Kyne Springs.

"I'll enlist the help of my family. We'll hire lawyers. The best. They can negotiate the return of the money you stole, and of course we will pay for the horse you killed too. Probably reimburse the county for the costs of the posse and my incarceration, and—"

"Don't be forgettin' you owe 'em for a new jailhouse window too," Liam said happily.

"I shall remind my lawyer of it, thank you. We'll pay for that too."

"Yer fam'bly will do all o' that, will they now?"

"Yes, they will."

He shook his head in a display of rapt admiration. "Think o' that, Boyd me son. 'Tis wonderful is what it is. An' these lawyers, they'll be gettin' the both o' us outa the hangman's reach?"

"I'm sure they will. I can almost promise it."

"That's grand, Boyd lad. It truly is."

"Liam."

"Aye?"

"There's something else I want to ask you."

"Anything, lad. Anything at all."

"You could've gotten away. Back there at the Pony Express station, I mean. The posse had me and never suspected your existence. You could just have ridden away."

Liam looked hurt. His near-constant grin faded dead away and he gave me a sad and even thoughtful look. "But boyo. We're friends."

I will tell you the truth. I had no response to that statement. Instead I got up and went to see if the hat was full again.

Chapter Thirty-four

"Oh, Danny Boy, the pipes, the pipes are ca-a-allin', from glen to glen an' down the mountain's side . . ."

"Aura Lee, Aura Lee . . ."

"She drove a wheelbarrow thru' streets broad an' narrow, singin' cockles an' mussels, alive, alive-o . . ."

"Bringing in the sheaves, bringing in the sheaves, we will go rejoicing, bringing in the sheaves . . ."

"All for me grog, boys, me jolly, jolly grog, all for me . . . hand me that bottle, will ye, lad? I've a thirst on for a nip to take the chill off, an' the singin' only brings it on the more."

I handed him the bottle. He kept passing it to me and out of politeness I would take a small sip each time, but the truth was that it was perfectly awful stuff and I didn't much care for it. I am not a prude, please understand, and have nothing against the enjoyment of spirits in moderation. But the key word there is enjoyment. This liquor that Liam had—gin, I believe it was—was most unpleasant to my taste however much he seemed to like it.

Still, it was a grand evening. We couldn't have a fire for

95

fear the posse might be able to see the light from it reflected on the rock walls above us. One might as well light a beacon as build a fire close by a rock face. But Liam had the foresight to lay in some supplies that did not need cooking. Jerked beef. A large chunk of smoked ham. Hard-boiled eggs. A poke heavy with corn dodgers. After the jailhouse grits I felt I was eating high on the hog, let me tell you.

And we had the pleasures of song.

Liam and I had learnt on that first evening we spent together that there was no point in attempting duets, for we simply did not know the same songs. But by the end of this evening each of us was learning enough of the other's favorites to join in now and then.

The sound of our combined voices, each of us being no more melodious than a steam engine's ear-piercing shriek, was something not to be believed. It amazed me that the poor horses did not burst their hobbles and escape into the desert in their anxiety to end the torture.

Liam and I, on the other hand, enjoyed the experience immensely. At least I did, and I believe that he did as well.

Liam took a deep swallow of the vile gin and handed the bottle back to me for my usual modest sip. Little though I was drinking, I was beginning to feel the effects of the alcohol. My cheeks tingled and the tip of my nose was becoming numb. And there was that most telling indicator of all—the gin was starting to taste good to me. This time I may have allowed a somewhat large measure to pass my lips.

"Let's try that 'Danny Boy' thing again, can we?"

"Aye, lad. D'you lead off now, an' I'll join in."

"Oh, Danny BOY, the pipes, the PIPES . . ."

It was a lovely evening. Posse, jailbreak, charges before the court, never mind any of that. This evening was simply lovely.

". . . and DOWN the mountainside . . ."

Chapter Thirty-five

I slept late. The sun was already over the horizon and shining into my closed eyes—it was this that woke me up, I think—before I stirred.

I yawned and sat up and thought longingly about coffee. I didn't know if Liam had brought any. And we still couldn't risk a fire even if he had. But oh, the desire was so strong I could almost taste the flavor of it on my tongue.

As it was, well, my mouth felt and tasted quite perfectly vile. I must have had more to drink than I'd realized.

Blinking and scratching, I looked around. Liam was up before me, I saw. The place where he'd spread his bed was empty now. He must've been . . .

The little son of a bitch!

He'd done it to me again.

Liam was gone.

The horses were gone.

Both horses were gone.

And my saddle was gone again too. With Uncle Edward's still-undiscovered money inside it. I hadn't been able to look beneath the lining, of course, not with Liam constantly close by, but I'd known from the weight of the saddle when I pulled it off the bay the previous evening that Uncle Edward's horse money was intact.

Now Liam had unknowingly stolen it again. Along with quite deliberately stealing my horse and saddle.

He'd taken my horse too because . . . I didn't know why he'd taken my horse as well as his. He just had. For whatever reason, he just had.

After breaking me out of jail. After restoring the horse and saddle to me. After such a grand evening of song and companionship.

Now he was gone. Again.

Damn him!

All I had left to me was a blanket.

And a posse trailing on horseback while I was afoot.

Oh, damn that miserable, low, rotten little Irishman anyway!

He'd left me nothing but . . . he'd left me the canteen. That surprised me. It lay beside the hollowed-out place I'd made to collect water in. The hat was there too. Liam's hat. He'd left that behind so, I suppose, I would not be without water.

Also a linen sack containing—I had to look—the beef jerky and corn dodgers.

At least the sorry little SOB hadn't intended me to starve or thirst to death.

Only, I suppose, to die by hanging if the posse caught up with me.

Damn him anyway.

I walked a little distance out into the desert, but I could see no sign of Liam or of the posse nor of any other living creature save a little sage and greasewood and the like. Not a cloud nor a bird in the sky, and not a snake nor a rabbit on the earth. I was alone. Penniless and without a horse, but with a posse and likely a death warrant seeking after me.

Believe me. I'd had better days.

Two

Chapter One

My feet hurt. My boots were cobbled for me by D. H. Birnie and Son in someplace nobody ever heard of called San Angelo, Texas, wherever that was—no, I'd never been there, but my cousin Beatrice made a pencil tracing around my foot so they would know the exact size and shape—and there were none better when it came to comfortable and long-lasting boots.

D. H. Birnie and Son has that reputation. For riding boots. I was not now riding. I was walking. Thanks to Mr. Liam O'Day, late of Ireland and if I ever caught up with him certain to be the late Mr. O'Day. Damn him!

My feet hurt from miles and miles of walking and they burned from the heat of the sun-scorched desert ground I walked over, and my thoughts burned even hotter every time I thought about the perfidious Liam O'Day and the horse he'd stolen from me. Twice.

Oh, I would fair have throttled that little man if I could only lay my hands upon him.

But I could not reach Liam O'Day and I could not reach any horse, and so I walked. On aching feet. Carrying my sack of eatables in one hand and with a nearly full canteen slung over my shoulder, the strap of which cut hard into my flesh and gave me pain there as well as in my poor, aching feet.

I did not like walking under any circumstance. God gave us dominion over horses and the other beasts of the field. Why would He have bothered doing that if He'd intended us to walk?

And across this dry and useless desert in the burning glare of day? I think not.

I know. I know. The accepted manner of crossing dry country afoot is to avoid the heat of day. To find shade and sleep in it through the day and then to walk at night. It's much more comfortable, much safer, and requires the use of far less water for the suffering soul who is afflicted with this necessity.

Had I only been trying to return home I would have done exactly that. Simply set my course northward bound and walked until I reached the railroad and eventually home. The problem with that was that Liam O'Day was quite obviously *not* intending to follow the program I'd laid out the previous evening.

He was going . . . I had no idea where he was going.

But wherever that was, I intended to go there too.

Mr. O'Day and I were not yet quits. He had my horse. He had my uncle's horse money.

And he had my dander up.

Liam delivered me from the hangman's noose, that may well be true, but he'd also abandoned me to a desperate fate and done it twice over.

I did most fully intend to discuss with him this breach of good manners.

In order to do this, of course, I had to once again find the miserable little rapscallion.

In order to find him, I had to follow him.

In order to follow him, I had to have daylight in which to track the two horses.

If there was danger in this from the posse that was sure to be behind, well, so be it.

If there was discomfort, even misery, from the heat and the sun and the pain in my feet, that was too bad.

I walked.

I grumbled.

It was just as well the womenfolk in the family could not overhear, for they would have been shocked to discover that I knew and was capable of using such language as I employed.

Damn that sorry little leprechaun anyway.

Chapter Two

Mistake. Big mistake. Boy, had I made one. Two. Two mistakes. Two mistakes that were killing me. Would've been better to hang. Least that would've been quick. This way . . . slow. Ugly.

I lay there. Dizzy. Weak. Couldn't walk. No shade. No water. Dying. But slow.

Two mistakes. First was the day thing. Trying to walk in day. Knew better, damn me. Knew I should walk at night. Wanted to track the little SOB Irishman. Wanted to follow. Had to see any sign. It was a mistake. Stupid.

Second one. Trying to go straight across desert. Should've stayed beside the mountain. Water there. Hidden sometimes, but there was water. Could've found it. Would've been all right. Walk north. To the railroad. Turn . . . what was it? Couldn't think. Dizzy. Vision blurry. North. That was it. To tracks. Turn left. Left. That's where home was. Go to tracks. Turn left. Family. Shamed. Lost Uncle Edward's money. But alive. God!

Lay there. Eyes shut. Couldn't see anyway. Nothing to see anyway. Sun burning down.

Funny thing. I wasn't sweating. I sweat a lot. Excuse me. Perspire. I perspire a lot generally. Not now. Dry as the dirt I was lying on. Hadn't sweat in . . . I don't know. Hours. Maybe not at all today.

This was . . . fourth day walking? Third? I wasn't sure anymore. It all ran together in my mind. Blurry, just like my vision.

Started out thinking to follow the leprechaun. Saw scrapes here and there. Now and then an upturned stone that showed a dark belly not yet bleached by exposure to the sun. Turned by a horse's hoof. Little things. Enough to let me know something—the leprechaun—came this way before me.

So I walked. I was strong. I had water and food. I could walk a long way.

Not long enough.

Too far. Just too far from the foothills where the thief camped with me and pretended to be my friend. Nothing but desert to the east. Faint lump in the distance, thin line low to the horizon. Next mountain over. Too far to see properly. And too low. O'Day knew, probably. Thought he could make it on a horse. Thought the posse wouldn't try. Give the little SOB his due. Probably thought I wouldn't try either. Not on foot.

Probably why he took both horses. A man can ride twice as far on two, right? Not really. But near enough to it that it wouldn't matter. Him on two horses. Posse with only one mount each. He could try to ride straight across this desert. The posse couldn't. And I?

I couldn't walk across it.

I knew that. Now.

Too late.

Lay there. Back burning from the sun. Eyes shut. Nothing to see anyway. Last time I looked, there wasn't but alkali flat and overhead some birds circling. Didn't know how many birds. I was seeing double by then anyway. Wasn't seeing anything now. Didn't want to look anyway.

Lucky damn birds. I was big. There'd be a lot for them to eat.

105

I would've cried, except there wasn't moisture enough in me for the tears.

All I could do was wait.

And die.

I couldn't cry. But I expect I sobbed more than a little and made believe that I was crying.

Join the Western Book Club
and GET 4 FREE* BOOKS NOW!
A $19.96 VALUE!

Yes! I want to subscribe to the Western Book Club.

Please send me my **4 FREE* BOOKS**. I have enclosed $2.00 for shipping/handling. Each month I'll receive the four newest Leisure Western selections to preview for 10 days. If I decide to keep them, I will pay the Special Members Only discounted price of just $3.36 each, a total of $13.44, plus $2.00 shipping/handling ($22.30 US in Canada). This is a **SAVINGS OF AT LEAST $6.00** off the bookstore price. There is no minimum number of books I must buy, and I may cancel the program at any time. In any case, the **4 FREE* BOOKS** are mine to keep.

*In Canada, add $5.00 shipping/handling per order for the first shipment. For all future shipments to Canada, the cost of membership is $22.30 US, which includes shipping and handling. (All payments must be made in US dollars.)

NAME: _____

ADDRESS: _____

CITY: _____ **STATE:** _____

COUNTRY: _____ **ZIP:** _____

TELEPHONE: _____

E-MAIL: _____

SIGNATURE: _____

Chapter Three

Angels. The angels were coming to carry me home. I could hear them whispering. Could feel their touch. Could feel myself float as they lifted me up. Their presence comforted me.

Their voices reached me faint but sweet through my distress.

". . . so sad."

". . . big fellow like . . ."

". . . help him, but . . ."

". . . stupid sonuvabitch!"

My body stiffened and I think my limbs spasmed a bit, and for half a heartbeat of time I thought I was falling.

"Whoa, goddammit!" The voice was neither faint nor sweet, and my heart lurched within me. These were not angels. I was being taken not up to home but to the other place.

The floaty feeling resumed, and after another moment or two the sun glare on my closed eyelids lessened and I felt a sharp bonk on the back of my head and heard the dull melon thump of the impact.

The demons were hauling me away in a conveyance of some sort.

If I'd had the tears to cry with I would have spilled my last remaining bits of moisture there and then.

Chapter Four

A cloth, cool and moist and cleansing, roved gently over my face and forehead. The touch of it woke me and brought me back from the distant place where I'd been.

I was not alone. A young woman bent over me with the cloth, which she continued to use to bathe my face and neck and hands. She didn't notice that I'd wakened, and so I had a few moments to study her.

She was not pretty in the conventional sense of things. Rather than pleasingly plump, she was thin, with hardly a spare ounce on her frame. Her face was lean, with hollowed cheeks beneath rather prominent cheekbones. Her eyebrows were heavy, her nose large, and her chin quite sharp.

Her hair and her eyes were dark. Day had turned into night while I slept and the light from a nearby fire was too faint to let me make out color, but I was more than a little startled to see that this young woman wore her hair hanging loose and full. It was a rather intimate sight. After all, I've grown up in a family with more girl cousins than boys and rarely have I seen any of them with their hair let down. I found the sight fairly shocking. Not unpleasant, mind. But a bit of a shock.

She turned to dip the cloth into a small basin of water again, wrung some of the excess moisture from it, and resumed bathing my face.

"Oh!" She jumped a little. "I didn't see . . . you're awake." She looked off to one side. "Papa. The man is awake now."

I tried to take stock of my surroundings, but I could see little. I seemed to be lying on the bed of a wagon of some sort, on the floor between rows of cabinetry built on either side of the rig. The roof and side walls were solid, not the usual canvas, and at the back there was a door instead of a tailgate. I'd never seen a wagon quite like it, the closest thing in my experience perhaps being a chuckwagon with its myriad compartments and purposed features. I lay in it now with my feet toward the door, my head toward whatever lay at the front. I did not have strength or at that moment inclination to make any further examination.

The firelight was masked by a form at the doorway, and a man appeared there. I could see little about him except that he seemed to be tall and as slender as his daughter and that he had pale hair and a thick beard.

"Good evening, son. I'm pleased you could join us." His voice was that of an orator, deep and rich and resonant.

"We were afraid you might die," the girl put in. It was not a novel thought, as of course I'd been quite convinced of it myself.

"Help him to sit up, dearie. I'll bring water."

Water. What a wonderful thought. My lips and throat were so dry that when I tried to greet and thank these people I had no power of speech whatsoever. The only sound to escape me was a faint croak.

The man lightly patted my leg and disappeared, allowing dancing yellow firelight into the doorway again.

The girl bent low and slipped an arm beneath my shoulders. With deceptive ease—for I was unable to do much to raise myself and must have been quite a burden—she lifted me to a sitting position.

The nearness of her when she did that was . . . unsettling. To say the least. In the cramped aisle of the wagon and with that particular task to accomplish, she had to place herself so close to me that I could feel the brush of her breath on my cheek. She smelled of licorice and wood smoke.

I'd never been so extraordinarily close to a woman before. Not even my own cousins. And the effect of her nearness was—should I confess to this—arousing as well as unsettling.

My breath caught somewhere inside my chest, and I could feel my heartbeat begin to race.

"There," she said. And without withdrawing, she smiled.

Her smile, seen so very close up, was quite dazzling.

There was at that moment—fortunately—a noise that distracted me and allowed me to regain some measure of dignity and self-control. I heard the sound of a barrel lid and the music of water spilling into a tin cup, and when the man came back he had water for me.

Water!

Thank you, Lord, I said silently as with a badly shaking hand I reached out for the life-giving fluid.

The girl saw and laid her hand over mine to help steady the cup and allow me to drink.

I'd never thought of water as having flavor. This water was sweeter and more welcome than any nectar could possibly have been.

Chapter Five

Between the two of them they helped me out of the wagon and to a seat close by a cheery blaze fed with chunks of ancient cedar collected, I supposed, from the mountainside above this camp, for we had come across the desert where they'd found me and were once more comfortingly close to something other than sun-bleached soil and strength-sapping wind.

I was shaky and so weak I doubt I could have stood without assistance, and I craved more water even after my belly was achingly full of it. Cup after cup, which the girl patiently filled and carried to me. It pleased me greatly to see that the dipper did not have to be lowered deep into their water barrel in order to fill itself.

Above the small barrel strapped to the side of the wagon, the moving light played over bright colors and gilt lettering. It took me a few moments to make out the exact wording, because the gilt paint—I seriously doubted they would have used actual gold leaf on so large an area—caught and reflected the firelight in such a way that it was difficult for me to see. Either that or my vision was still as weak as my body, but I do believe it was the light and not myself that was at fault there.

In any event, the lettering blazoned in an arc across the full length of the wagon read: "Professor Baltzer Burdash's Belladonna Balm, Secret of the Mysterious Orient, Elixir of Kings and Potentates, Energizing Restorative Tonic."

All of this was, you will understand, arranged in several lines or levels of display so that all would fit and the letters yet be made large.

The gentleman—I'd first thought he was blond but now saw that his hair was gray—must have seen me trying to work out the wording on his wagon. And he must also, I would assume, have decided that I was either uneducated or slow of wit when in fact I was merely at pains to see because of the uncertain firelight. For whatever reason, he slowly and carefully read out the content of the wording for me, concluding with. "And I, young man, am Professor Baltzer Burdash. In person. Master of these Oriental mysteries."

These. He said "these" mysteries. Only one was mentioned on the sign that he was quoting. Even so . . .

"And this," the rich and sonorous voice went on, "is the Princess Zarah."

She'd called him "papa" when she told him I was awake. I remembered that distinctly. Still, who was I to question these people. They'd saved me from certain death. It would not be seemly now for me to look into their relationship. Whatever it might be.

And if it were something other than a blood tie . . . well, I could not fault a man for finding Princess Zarah appealing. There was something about her, some quality or aura or . . . I cannot begin to describe it any more than I could hope to comprehend it. But whatever it was, it was powerful.

There in the shifting light she indeed did look exotic. And mysterious. And a princess.

I was so full of water I feared my belly would soon burst. But I held out my cup to Princess Zarah, and she took it and stood and returned to the water barrel yet one more time, her movements fluid and graceful, her wrists tiny and delicate, her neck impossibly long and slender, her waist nearly nonexistent, and her . . . never mind. The rest did not bear thinking upon.

"Thank you," I said when she handed me the refilled cup.

"You are most welcome." Her voice was throaty and rather low in pitch. Or is that tone? I tend to get those mixed up. Husky, let us say. Her voice was husky. Very odd for a woman.

I strained to recognize any hint of accent in her English, reasoning that just as you can hear the remnants of foreign tongues in a man's speech when you encounter a Basque, say, or a Mexican or an Indian, surely Princess Zarah would have some lingering traces of her own native language when she spoke now. But I could make out nothing of the sort. Except for that husky quality in her voice, her English was quite as good as my own.

I sipped very, very slowly at the water, wishing I hadn't taken quite so much of it already so that I could still hold more. And ask yet again to observe as Princess Zarah floated to and from Professor Burdash's gaudy medicine wagon.

I was, I would have to admit, quite thoroughly entranced.

I was also, dagnabbit, becoming quite thoroughly uncomfortable.

All of that water—forgive me if I am indelicate here—all of that water could not be absorbed so rapidly by the body's tissues, not even ones so parched as mine, and it, ahem, had to go somewhere.

I squirmed. Wriggled. Suffered acute pains in the bladder. Something had to give. Soon. And it had to be me.

"Sir," I ventured, turning my face from the girl.

"Yes, young man?"

"Could you help me to my feet, sir? I do not believe I can manage it on my own."

"Is something wrong? I was just about to offer you something to eat. Are you all right?"

"Papa! Really. The gentleman has to pee. Now help him." She laughed. "Unless you want me to."

The professor laughed. Princess Zarah laughed. I thought I might have been better off dying in the desert.

But I accepted help from both of them to get me upright once again.

Chapter Six

I got something of a shock—well, maybe it was more on the order of a surprise than an actual shock—when I was standing on my own hind legs again. Professor Burdash and Princess Zarah got one on either side to help me up, and once they did I found myself looking *up* by a couple inches to the professor and almost eye to eye with the princess.

Mind, now, I stand just shy of six and a half feet myself. Professor Burdash was several inches taller and Princess Zarah, I guessed, would have to be six feet two or thereabouts.

I hadn't noticed that before, what with one distraction or another, but now it struck me.

And for some perverse reason I, whose measure of feminine pulchritude has always been—excuse me for admitting this, but it is true—back-bar depictions of short, plump women with nothing but perhaps a thin draping of silk scarf failing to conceal their, um, charms . . . I found this tall, lean, physically strong young woman from God knew what distant land . . . I found her immensely attractive. Exciting. Exotic. Intoxicating.

That, however, had *nothing* to do with my loss of balance. That mishap I blame solely on my weak and debilitated condition after so nearly thirsting to death in the south Nevada desert.

Due to this and this only, I experienced one of those bouts of sudden and severe dizziness such as one sometimes has when standing too abruptly.

I lost my balance entirely and fell. Sideways. Onto Princess Zarah. Who reached to steady and hold me.

My weight taken so unexpectedly was too much for her, and we both fell to the ground.

I ended up lying half on top of her, with the startled professor looming over us.

I, of course, was mortified.

The professor was alarmed.

Princess Zarah was laughing.

It was too much. I scrambled onto all fours and backed away like an overlarge spider, then jumped to my feet as quickly and easily as a calf coming off its bedground, unmindful of anything save a great desire to enter the darkness beyond the firelight's reach.

Weak? Dizzy? I had no thought for either of those. My humiliation was too complete to admit them room for thought.

I hurried away to conclude the need that precipitated this unpremeditated assault, leaving the professor to play the gallant and help Princess Zarah to her feet.

But, oh my, lean though she was the princess was almighty soft to the touch.

I carried indelibly with me now memories of both the feel and the scent of her, and together they fair made my head to swim.

Chapter Seven

"And what, may I ask, is your name, sir?"

It was a question you'd think a fellow would be prepared to answer. After all, these folks saved my life. They'd been free with their own names, with their water, now with their food. So the question was an ordinary enough one.

It was also one I hadn't bothered to give thought to. Until it was asked. I can, you see, be blind to the perfectly obvious sometimes. And of course they would ask that simple question of me.

But . . . how to answer? It was still far from being known how this business would turn out. My family could yet be disgraced by my behavior. Especially so now that I'd participated—willingly—in an escape from the Lewis County jail. I could plead innocence and circumstance to all which went before that. But not to the escape. When Liam ripped half the courthouse wall out, or so it sounded at the time, I went in that instant from victim to perpetrator. It changed things greatly.

Because of this I was more than ever concerned with protecting the name and reputation of the family.

Telling these fine people the simple truth was out of the question.

Giving them my already established nom de guerre seemed equally unwise. After all, there was a posse out there somewhere that almost certainly was still in pursuit of Liam O'Day and of myself. They were in search of someone named Robert Boyd. So it seemed inadvisable to claim that name, for who knew what rumors would be told or stories circulated or—far worse—rewards posted for the capture of the vicious, jailbreaking, bank-robbing, safe-blowing-up desperado Bob Boyd. No, that name had run its course for me.

But . . . what to answer now?

And how long could I sit there with a blank and silly expression trying to determine a fit response to the professor's gentle probing?

I stuffed a spoonful of bland, watery, and in truth rather unpleasant stew into my mouth to give me an excuse for delaying my answer.

"Michael," I said once I'd swallowed. That name came to mind because of my certainty that the Archangel Michael would surely strike me dead even if the posse failed to find and hang me. I was, after all, no longer the respectable person who'd ridden so lightheartedly from home those scant few weeks earlier.

"Stew," I added, looking at the bowl in my hand, ". . . art."

"Pardon me?"

"Stewart, sir. Michael Stewart." It wasn't a grand name perhaps, but it would do.

"You appear to be feeling better, Michael."

"Yes, sir, thanks to you and Princess Zarah."

He waved the gratitude aside. "The least we could do, Michael. It was nothing."

"Not to me, sir."

"Would you care for more stew, Michael?" Princess Zarah asked.

"This is plenty, thank you." More than plenty, in a manner of speaking. It may have been several days since I'd eaten, but, well, the straight and narrow of it was that Princess Zarah was beautiful and alluring but she was *not* a good cook. Even I could do better, and I am no cook at all.

Once the twin unpleasantnesses of name-giving—name inventing, that is—and supper were safely out of the way the remainder of the evening passed agreeably enough. I helped Princess Zarah with the washing up, then bedded down close by the fire on a blanket supplied by my host and hostess. The water and food revived me considerably, but I still had some way to go toward regaining my strength.

And I did expect to need my strength again.

Liam O'Day was still out there somewhere with Uncle Edward's horse money inside the saddle he'd twice stolen from me.

I'd neither forgotten nor forgiven, and so long as breath remained in my body I would be after him like a feist dog after a squirrel. No. Forget that. Dogs seldom ever actually catch a squirrel, and my goal was not the chase but the capture thereafter.

I went to sleep that night with my thoughts aswirl, leaping willy-nilly from Liam O'Day to Princess Zarah and rudely back again.

Chapter Eight

"I take it that you and the princess travel, sir," I idly commented as we bumped and rattled along a track that was no road but which at least showed sign it had been traveled by wheeled vehicles in the past.

"Indeed we do, Michael. Princess Zarah and I bring succor to the afflicted throughout this land."

"With the, um, tonic as mentioned on your signs," I said. I was seated beside the professor. Princess Zarah remained inside the wagon now that there was need to accommodate a third passenger in the vehicle. There would have been room enough in the driving box for all three of us, but it would have been crowded. In truth, I would have liked that. If you take my meaning. Unfortunately, the princess chose to remain inside the wagon rather than wedge herself between the professor and me.

"With Professor Burdash's Belladonna Balm, yes. It is a most wonderful curative, Michael. Restores one's energy. Settles the stomach. Oh, yes, it is little short of being miraculous. We also offer our customers—I prefer to think of them as patients actually—another truly soothing and ef-

121

fective Oriental medication known as Whitford's Effica-
cious Salve."

"Whitford's Effi—"

"A most wonderful product, Michael. When applied ex-
ternally it relieves aching and deep pain in joint or muscle.
Speeds healing of open wounds. And has a most pleasant
odor, unlike most less effective competing products. Would
you care to try some, Michael?"

"No, sir. I'm pretty well free of joint pain or open wounds
at the moment, thank you."

"Would you like to sample Professor Burdash's Belladonna Balm, then?"

"Well, I—"

"Papa!" Princess Zarah's voice reached quite sharply forward through the window that allowed air to pass into the
body of the wagon. "It's early in the day."

"I only intended giving the young gentleman a sample,"
the professor said without bothering to turn his head. Out
in front the near horse flicked its ears and lifted its head,
probably responding to the professor's louder voice with
the thought the team—an exceptionally handsome pair of
heavy-bodied grays—was about to be asked for a change of
gait. When no such demand was forthcoming, the animal
blew snot and shook itself but never faltered in its brisk and
regular trot.

"No samples this early," Princess Zarah called.

"Yes, dear." The professor winked at me and reached beneath the driving seat to rummage with one hand into a
canvas bag he carried there. He withdrew a small, brown
glass bottle that would hold, I judged, half a pint or so of
liquid. The bottle had no label or other markings on it and
was nearly full.

The professor laid a cautionary finger over his lips to en-
sure my silence, then pulled the cork and handed the bottle
to me for a taste.

I couldn't question the contents, not at that moment
when Princess Zarah might overhear, but did take a moment to sniff of the exotic elixir. It smelled of licorice and

. . . something else. I couldn't quite identify the something else.

Still, I doubted these nice folk would have rescued me from the desert only to kill me with the means of their livelihood. I raised the bottle to my lips and let a small amount trickle into my mouth.

The taste was not unpleasant. A little hot on the tongue. And when I swallowed there was a warm and gentle glow that spread through my stomach. Alcohol. The elixir most definitely contained a liberal quantity of alcohol. Which probably explained why Princess Zarah objected to its early-day usage.

Even so—and I'd been quite frankly skeptical when I sampled the product—even so there was a marked effect, just as the professor said. Within minutes I felt more alert. Much more energetic. The professor's elixir quickened my pulse and sharpened my mind and made me feel quite peppy indeed.

Unfortunately, by that time the professor had helped himself to a sample of his own product and returned the bottle to the underseat bag.

If he offered me another taste, I concluded, next time it would be a larger one than a single sip.

The professor winked at me again and shook his driving lines a bit to capture the attention of his horses, then pulled them down from the trot to a walk as the way before us rose onto a slight grade leading to another of the interminable low hogback ridges that fanned out toward the desert from the spine of arid mountain that flanked us to the east, on the left side as we traveled slowly southward.

Chapter Nine

"May I ask you something, sir?" I ventured.

"Of course, Michael." Michael. It was going to take me a while to become accustomed to that name.

"Where are we bound, Professor?" I could tell from the rise and fall of the sun what direction we took, of course, but I had no earthly idea of where we were nor where we might be headed. And while riding it had occurred to me that if the professor and princess were en route to Lewisville Flats it might be wise for me to, um, excuse myself from their company.

"A fair enough question, Michael. The town is known as Pleasant Prospect."

I'd never heard of it. "Is that in Nevada, sir?"

"To the best of my knowledge it is, yes."

"Strange name for a town in the middle of all this," I said, waving in a general sort of way toward the dry and barren desert we passed through.

"It was the name that attracted me to it," the professor admitted. "We have not been there before."

"Is that what you do? Drive from town to town to sell your wares?"

"Exactly so, Michael. We carry with us copious quantities of healing and diversion. We serve no master but fate, follow no path but our own. Princess Zarah and I are free, Michael. Truly free. We bring joy and take away naught but a meager few alms." The professor nodded and, as if he'd just reminded himself of his own Belladonna Balm, reached beneath the seat for another nip out of the little bottle.

This time when he offered it to me I had no hesitation. Between us we lowered the level of the contents by a fair amount.

Chapter Ten

Pleasant Prospect was . . . not very pleasant. And didn't look like it had much in the way of prospects, either.

It was barely big enough to call itself a town even by Nevada standards, where it doesn't take much more than a good-sized cow camp to start a town. Pleasant Prospect had maybe two dozen houses and half a dozen stores. Plus, of course, five—I counted—saloons. But then, just the fact that the town existed and had some places where you could buy or at least order goods from elsewhere would be draw enough to bring folks in off the desert for fifty, sixty miles around.

There would be browse enough somewhere in all that wide sweep of land to carry a few head of cows or some sheep or some goats. And off to the south the glare of bright sun off starkly white flats suggested there would be salt down there to mine.

The track Professor Burdash was following came down from the north and continued off to the south somewhere out past the salt flats, and there was a much better traveled road that intersected it, that one running east and west.

That would be the regular freight and stagecoach route, I should think, linking California with Arizona and Texas and all those other places in the east that I'd likely never see but only read about.

"I suppose you will want to leave us here, Michael," the professor said as we rolled nearer to Pleasant Prospect. "I for one will certainly miss you. I've enjoyed your company. And your help with the team and wagon."

We'd been together now for four days—well, four that I was awake enough to know anything about, that is—and naturally enough I'd taken over the horses and the camp chores. The professor wasn't either especially young nor especially spry, and anyway helping out was the least I could do after him and Princess Zarah went and saved my life back there.

And I do mean the *least*, for I hadn't a shinplaster penny in my pockets to pay them with. Liam O'Day had stolen Uncle Edward's money, and the traveling money I'd had in my pockets and in my saddlebags was back there in the Lewis County jail along with pretty much everything else I'd owned.

The professor swung the wagon off to the east a way before he reached the better road and turned onto it. I couldn't see why he would do that at first. Then I realized, for when we rolled onto the main street where the few store buildings were lined up I heard a noise from in the back of the wagon.

There was music coming from back there, by golly. It was faint but unmistakable, and it drew more than just my attention, for almost immediately heads began to pop out of doorways and windows to see what was happening here.

The professor shook the driving lines and made a little chirping sound, and the grays began to toss their heads and prance just as handsome as you please.

The music—it was one of those hand-crank grinder organ things, or whatever you call them—was being played by Princess Zarah, of course, although nobody in Pleasant Prospect would know that, for she was keeping herself out of sight in the back of the wagon.

127

The professor took us down the entire length of the town—not that there was so awful much distance involved, but his purpose was clear enough—and drew to a halt just beyond the last commercial building on the street, it being a mercantile that also had a large corral laid out behind it. A fading sign painted onto the far wall of the store building advertised hay, grain, and wheel repairs, so I guessed this would be where the teamsters and coachmen traded.

"Michael."

"Yes, sir?"

"Would you be kind enough to help me set up for our, uh, presentation here? Princess Zarah and I are perfectly capable of doing it ourselves. But I believe it would be nice if she could remain unseen for the time being. Would you do that before you take your leave of us?"

"I would do anything for you, sir. Anything."

"Excellent, Michael. Thank you." He turned and in a low voice warned Princess Zarah to remain where she was. In a soft voice, because by now there were half a dozen or so small boys pressing close beside the wagon, peering at the professor most of all but at me too and at the high-stepping grays and at the side of the wagon where the gilt lettering stood out bold and shiny in the sunshine.

"Good day, young gentlemen," the professor called out cheerily. "Good day and welcome to you. Are your parents aware of my arrival, lads? Will you tell them for me? But wait, now. Don't rush off. Here." He bent down and picked up the poke where he kept that sample bottle of Professor Burdash's Belladonna Balm.

I was concerned for a moment that he was going to pass some of the elixir to the children. And while it was dandy stuff—the small bottle we'd first sampled was long since empty, but there proved to be plenty more where that one came from—I did not believe it suitable for children.

I needn't have worried. Professor Burdash fetched out a linen bag, unfastened the drawstring that held it closed, and began handing out horehound candies.

If he wanted an attention-getter—as he most surely did— that was the icing on the cake. Children who'd been hanging back and watching from a distance came leaping and bounding to claim their share of this bounty, and I do not for a moment doubt that in the next two or three minutes the professor had pressed candy into the hands of each and every child in the town. Some of them twice, for I recognized two freckled youngsters who came back for seconds.

"All right, now. That is enough. Be good enough to tell your parents about my arrival, if you please."

Not that he really needed to say that, for the clamoring of the children had brought the town's grown-ups out onto the street and the few sidewalks where they were observing all of this.

"I shall make my presentation shortly before sundown," Professor Burdash called out in his rich, booming voice. "Tell one, tell all. The mysteries of the Orient shall be unveiled. Tell one, tell all. Sundown it shall be."

The professor watched the children scamper off to their homes like a covey of quail taking flight. Then he turned and gave me a wink. "Watch and learn, Michael. Watch and learn."

Chapter Eleven

Getting them ready for their . . . presentation, as the professor termed it, proved to be somewhat more of a task than I'd expected. From beneath the wagon box came six sturdily constructed wooden, well, *things*. They looked like heavy crates that the side pieces fell off, but the professor placed them with considerable care and measuring in two rows at the back of the wagon and running perpendicular to it, forming a T shape there, if you will. He had several lengths of carpenter's cord that helped him get the exact placement that he wanted.

I didn't understand this procedure. But then, the good thing was that I didn't have to. I simply supplied the muscle to carry and place the things while the professor told me where each went.

When we were done, however, I thought I understood. The now-upright crates formed a rectangle about the same size as the wagon itself but, as I said, perpendicular to it.

"And now, Michael, would you please help me with the part of this that Princess Zarah and I find difficult. The roof, lad, is partly false front. We carry our stage floor up there.

Would you be kind enough to lift the pieces down for me."

Which explained the rest of this small mystery. I stood on the driving seat and from there could see that the roof of the wagon indeed held broad, thick slabs of lumber in an assortment of sizes.

Once brought down—it would have been a perfectly awful job for a gentleman of the professor's years with only a girl to help him—these were quickly assembled over the top of the platform stands, as those crate-looking things proved to be, to form an acceptably sturdy stage at the back of the wagon reinforced with steel pins that the professor slipped through prepositioned holes in the lumber pieces to firmly connect each with the framework and platform stands below.

Poles that had been suspended beneath the wagon were erected and a scarlet red canvas shade draped over them, so now there was not only a stage platform, this stage was roofed.

A curtain was rigged across the back of the wagon to act as a backdrop to the stage as well.

It all fit together with cunning precision, and I had to marvel at the cleverness of the arrangement. Where minutes before stood only a fairly ordinary-looking wagon now there was an actual stage.

The professor disappeared inside the now-curtained door of the wagon and emerged shortly with some reflector lamps, four of them, which he bolted onto the front of the stage facing inward.

"When we are ready to commence, Michael, I would like for you to light these and make sure their light is directed onto me."

"Yes, sir."

"And if you would be so good, please help me bring out the boxes of my elixir and Whitford's salve, will you?"

"Of course, Professor."

He handed out several quite heavy wooden crates and directed me where to pile them at the rear of the stage area.

"Now, Michael, would you be kind enough to see to the

livestock for me. I shall in the meanwhile prepare myself for our, um, presentation, eh?"

"Shall I put them in the corral over there, sir? The horses, I mean?"

"Where? Oh. Yes, I see. There is water there?"

"Yes, sir. Or at least I see a trough."

"That would be splendid, Michael. And tell whoever is in charge that I shall pay for whatever hay they consume if any is available."

"Yes, sir."

The professor went inside the now quite transformed wagon while I led the grays to the corral gate and took them inside. The handful of other horses already there, standing hipshot and sleepy-eyed in the slanting afternoon sunlight, naturally stirred themselves enough to come near so they could inspect these newcomers to their small and temporary herd.

I was midway through removing the collar from the off horse when my breath caught in my throat and I began to tremble.

For one of the horses in that corral was the handsome black that Liam O'Day stole back in Lewisville Flats.

Chapter Twelve

I hurried through the rest of the needs of the grays, not giving them as thorough a currying as they deserved after their day's work but anxious to speak with whoever owned this enclosure.

Inside the adjacent mercantile I found a swarthy man with a huge mustache and an egg-bald scalp leaning on the counter.

"Those are your horses in my corral?" Obviously he'd seen me out there with them.

"Professor Burdash's, actually," I told him.

"Ten cents each. Grain would be extra if he wants any."

"I'll ask him about that, sir. May I ask you, though, about the tall black horse I noticed in the bunch."

"Is he yours?" the storekeeper countered. Which seemed a strange enough question.

"I . . . no, sir. Why would you ask?"

"Fellow came through here two days ago and said he found the animal wandering loose on the road. He said surely anyone who owned an animal of that quality would be looking for him and asked if I'd be willing to let the horse stay here until the owner shows up. Even gave me a dollar toward the feed and water until or unless. If no one claims him I suppose I'd sell him eventually. But it wouldn't be right for me to take any offers on him at least until he's eaten up that dollar. Another eight days, call it. Are you interested?"

"I might be," I said just as calmly as I knew how, even though I could still feel the blood pounding in my ears. "Does he have any tack with him?"

"In the corner over there is what he was wearing when this Good Samaritan found him."

I looked. And my hopes fell. It was the saddle Liam stole along with the black that lay in an untidy heap on the floor. My saddle—and Uncle Edward's money—were still on my bay with Liam O'Day. Wherever he was.

But whyever would O'Day have abandoned the black? Could Liam have been captured by the posse from Lewisville Flats? Or might something—an accident . . . a gunfight—some such thing have happened to Liam? My bay and saddle could be wandering loose somewhere in the brush if so.

"This man who found the horse, could I talk to him?"

"He isn't from around here, I'm afraid, and he never gave me his name. Someone over at the Calliope might know it, though. He spent most of yesterday there, or so I hear. Nice fellow. And uncommonly honest. Most would've kept a horse like that one or sold it to me. I wouldn't've known different if he said he wanted to sell it."

"I'm sure that's true, sir. Uh, since I don't have this gentleman's name, perhaps you could tell me how I should ask for him at the . . . Calliope, did you say?"

"The Calliope is the saloon across the street and two buildings down. Just ask about the little redheaded Irishman. They're sure to know who you mean."

"Irish," I repeated.

"That's right. Brogue thick as a blanket. Tiny wee little fellow. Always smiling. Rides a great big bruiser of a bay horse. Little as he is, he makes quite a sight atop such a big horse, let me tell you. You just ask Harry about the Irishman. And tell him Stavros sent you, so he doesn't think you wish that nice little man harm."

"Harry would be the gentleman who runs the Calliope?"

"That's right. And I am Stavros."

"Yes, sir. Thank you very much, sir."

Honest little Irishman, I was muttering to myself as I left the mercantile. Honest! Miserable little thief is what he was. Thief. Liar. There weren't enough bad things one might say about him that would fully cover the subject.

But I thought I had a good idea of why he would have left the black here in Pleasant Prospect like that. The members of the posse that was chasing him—chasing us, that is—had no idea who broke me out of that jail. None of them ever saw Liam in the commission of that particular crime, just as none of them saw him when he blew that safe and burgled their bank.

By leaving the horse for its rightful owner, even if he were caught Liam could claim innocence. Someone else robbed the bank. Someone else engineered the jailbreak. Someone else stole that horse.

Why did I have the distinct and unpleasant notion that when push came to shove, I would be the one left holding the bag for all those crimes and probably more?

It certainly worked out that way so far, anyway.

I stepped outside and glanced toward the rapidly setting sun. There was probably more the professor needed. But I did most sorely want to have a brief word with this Harry person at the Calliope Saloon.

I broke into a shambling trot in the direction of the saloon. People were already beginning to drift toward the professor's wagon, and I was needed back there to light the lamps and do whatever else was required. Besides, if I hoped to have anything in the way of a supper tonight it would pretty much have to be taken with the professor and Princess Zarah, as I had neither money to buy a meal nor time enough to work for one.

So I hied myself off to the Calliope with all the speed I could manage.

Chapter Thirteen

I was puffing like a leaky steam engine by the time I got back to the transformed wagon, having run as fast as I was able all the way from the Calliope Saloon. Such a crowd had gathered that the merchants were closing their stores and coming to join everyone else. They might just as well anyway, for the entire town was turned out in front of the professor's stage. I estimated there must have been more than a hundred folk of all ages, even the ladies. Entertainment, I gathered, was a rare commodity in Pleasant Prospect.

I hurried around them to the front of the wagon to find the tin box where the professor kept the sulfur matches he used to light the cooking fire evenings and then back to the stages so I could light the lamps as he'd requested.

By this time the dusk was thick and the heat of the day moderated. My belly growled with hunger, but there was no time for that.

The lamps brought the stage to a state of amazing brightness against the relative dark all around. Something I noticed with some surprise was that once the lamps were lighted and turned upon the stage to isolate as well as illuminate it, the faces in the crowd seemed to meld all together. It was as if the crowd became one entity rather than a collection of so many individuals. I cannot explain that. But from my place there beside the stage at the front of it all I could sense it.

The professor, of course, must have been waiting for me to perform my one tiny role in this affair for as soon as I'd lighted the lamps and stepped to the side, the scarlet curtain parted and the professor stepped through.

And not only was the wagon transformed, so was the professor. Where before he'd been a tall old man in traveling clothes, now he was . . . a performer. And a powerfully captivating one at that.

He wore now a boiled shirt and celluloid collar, a bright yellow neckerchief—necktie, I believe some call this fashion—cutaway swallowtail coat, gray silk vest, and, most impressive of all, a stovepipe silk hat. The old man was tall to begin with, and between the elevation of the stage and that hat, he now positively towered above the commonplace mortals below.

He impressed me. And I knew the sounds of his passing wind in the night. The impression he made upon the townspeople of Pleasant Prospect must have been immense. Calculatedly so, of course. My hat was off to the old gentleman. He knew his business indeed.

"Gentlemen. Ladies. Fellow wayfarers on this journey through life. I have come among you this delectable evening to bring you health and a fuller measure of life's enjoyment. From far Siam and the jungles of fearsome Tasmania I bring to you the mysteries of the Orient, dear friends. I bring to you . . ."

Oh, it was quite something the way the professor orated. In that rich voice which seemed as if it must have been predestined for such purpose as this, he lectured and informed. He stalked the boards from one side to another. His words rose and fell in volume like sheets of wind sweeping across an oat field. Soft, then loud, sometimes even harsh.

He spoke of places and of things scarcely to be imagined. Elephants and tigers and mountains so high their peaks were sheathed in perpetual cloud and in six generations had not been seen by human eye.

He spoke of snakes and camels and naked Hindu fakirs.

And he spoke finally of a mystic named Bargaloo whom Professor Burdash once rescued from a death by drowning and who in gratitude shared with the professor the greatest of his secrets.

A secret, the professor said, he was now willing to share with the world.

A secret, the professor said, that brought him here in his quest to deliver all mankind from lethargy and ill health.

A secret he . . . But he was becoming weary. Would these good people excuse him. He himself felt the need to resort to the medicinal qualities of this most perfect restorative.

With their permission, he said, he would retire for a brief moment. And while he did so, while he recouped his flagging energies, he would call upon the services of one more wonder brought here from the temples of Siam to demonstrate one of the hidden rites in an appeal to the heathen gods for prosperity.

With that the professor withdrew behind the curtain.

There was a rustling of the cloth, a poking and prodding of the material, but for the moment nothing else.

The crowd began to grow slightly restive. Murmuring could be heard as people nudged their neighbors and began to whisper. They'd come here to be entertained, not to peer at an empty stage.

This delay, I discovered, was entirely deliberate. A matter of preparation, if you will.

For when that curtain did part, Princess Zarah—whose presence remained heretofore unsuspected—appeared in the spotlight.

I'd thought the professor transformed?

My breath caught in my throat when I now beheld Princess Zarah, and I scarcely recognized her as first my savior and next my genial companion of these last few days.

Princess Zarah was . . . stunning. Not a whit less than stunning.

Chapter Fourteen

Princess Zarah was every bit as exotic and stunning as her name implied. She did genuinely seem a princess. And from a place where things are vastly different from the way we might know them here. She showed . . . well, her actual *ankles* were displayed. Unclothed. Completely.

It was shocking. I heard a gasp from the massed crowd behind me. I may have made such a sound myself.

Her costume was . . . May I use the term "exotic" yet again? For truly it was.

Her hair flowed long and free, but I'd come to accept this as her normal manner of wearing it. But now it was contained by a bright red silk scarf tied around her forehead, the ends long and left to hang free at the back, where it was in stark contrast to the jet of her gleaming hair.

She wore earrings of hammered gold disks like small coins linked together into a string, the smallest at the top and each succeeding one below slightly larger until the bottom-most was the size of a half dollar or so. Together they probably extended five or six inches, dangling and jangling and catching the light with every motion or movement.

Frank Roderus

A thin cord held a wisp of translucent fabric of some sort suspended like an apron—a veil, I suppose one would say—that masked much of her face. The veil, in a shade of red not quite so striking as the scarf, hid her nose and mouth and jaw from view but served to emphasize her eyes, which were outlined with a substance as dark as bootblack, while her eyelids—I found this quite incredible indeed—were coated with a powdery green substance that actually glittered in the focused glare of the footlights.

Beneath all this she wore a snow-white shirtwaist partially covered but in truth emphasized by a very short black vest that did not close over her, uh, bosom but instead was joined at the front by three golden chains that left a gap of several inches where the white of the shirtwaist showed.

And beneath this was the most amazing garment of all.

She wore *trousers*!

Actual trousers. But wholly unlike any trousers I ever saw before.

These were made of a cloth so light and thin I almost—not quite, but almost—thought I could see right through it. In fact, had the lights been behind her . . . well, I can hardly imagine the resultant view. Did not at that moment *want* to give such freedom to my imagination. It would have been altogether too disturbing.

This cloth was cut tight to the waist and hips, while the trouser legs flared full and loose and wide so that they could swirl and sway almost as if skirts. This wide and flowing effect continued down to the lower calf, where they became narrow and tight again.

And below that *she wore nothing at all*.

Below those trousers—or pantaloons, I suppose they might be called—Princess Zarah's ankles and feet were—please excuse my use of the word, but it is accurate—naked. Genuinely, truly, utterly naked.

No wonder the crowd, myself included, gasped so.

And on her toes—not everyone was close enough to see this, perhaps, but I at the very front had an unobstructed view—on her toes there were rings. Golden rings. Just like one might wear on a finger. Except these rings were on her toes.

I'd never . . . I was going to say I'd never heard of such a thing before, but of course I had. In a nursery rhyme I'd learnt as a child there was something about "rings on her fingers, rings on her toes, and she will have" something, I could no longer remember what, "wherever she goes."

Princess Zarah was a fantasy come to life.

Good heavens!

From inside the wagon I could hear music now. That would be the professor, of course. It was another of those hand-crank devices making the music, some tune I'd never heard before.

And Princess Zarah began to sway in time with it. Then she raised her arms. She clicked her fingers and clapped her hands.

Her hips moved and her arms swept high and from side to side.

Her feet, her bare feet, stamped and spun.

She twirled. Swirled. Pirouetted and spun in whirling circles.

She pointed to the heavens and beckoned unseen forces. Her movements enticed and invited and soon commanded all who might watch.

Heathen? Certainly. Mystic? Without doubt.

But oh, the effect.

By the time the music had ended and Princess Zarah had slipped discreetly behind the curtain once more, I daresay there was not a man in the community not present at the back of that wagon. Nor a child who remained. All of them had been grasped firmly and dragged away by their shocked and horrified mothers.

It was amazing. Yet despite my own fascination with that close view of Princess Zarah at work, I had to admire Professor Burdash all the more.

For in this manner he had without a single word of command brought to him the exact audience he proposed to attract. And no other.

I admired the man for this.

And despised him for so allowing Princess Zarah to be placed on display where crude and vulgar men might be tempted into lewd or lecherous contemplation.

I remained where I was, of course. I might yet be needed for some purpose. Besides, Princess Zarah could well return to the stage, and if she did I intended still to be there in my best of all possible positions for viewing.

But my feelings were mixed about it all, and my mind troubled. I scarcely noticed when the professor returned, and had little attention to give his spiel from that point onward.

Chapter Fifteen

"Thank you for helping so much, Michael," the professor said. It was late now, probably approaching midnight. But the stage had all been disassembled and everything packed away again and the water barrels refilled. "I should like to pay you something for your services."

"No, sir. I couldn't take anything from you. Not after what you and Princess Zarah have done for me. I wouldn't feel right about it." And I meant that, even though I knew quite good and well that he could afford to pay me if I chose to accept. He must have taken in more than forty dollars, just from this tiny crowd. The earning potential in a larger community I could scarcely imagine.

"Are you sure?"

"Yes, sir, but I do thank you for the offer."

"Will you be leaving us now?" he asked.

I guess I hesitated just a bit too long, not certain how I should answer that.

"You are a big help to us, Michael. It is especially good that with your strong hands we can get set up without any-one suspecting Zarah's presence. It's ever so much more

143

effective when she can expose herself for the first time like she did this evening, believe me."

"I'd like to stay with you, sir." And that was certainly the truth. "It's just . . . have you decided which direction you'll be taking in the morning?"

"I haven't thought about it. Does it make a difference to you, Michael?"

"Yes, sir, it does."

"We travel without itinerary, Michael. Which direction would you prefer?"

"South, sir," I said firmly. For that was the direction the saloon keeper at the Calliope Saloon said Liam O'Day had taken. And rode out just yesterday at that. On *my* bay horse.

"South?" The professor shrugged. "I've no objection to driving south. Do you know the next town in that direction?"

"No, sir."

"But you've a reason to go there?"

"Yes, sir, I do."

"Would you care to share that reason with us?"

I had to pause again in an attempt to collect my thoughts. I owed these people my very life. But . . . I was a wanted felon. Perhaps even with a price on my head. I trusted them. Of course I did. Up to a point. The thing was, I had no idea where that point should be placed. And anyway, they might be wary of me if I admitted to them any part of my true circumstance.

How many, after all, would care to travel with someone accused of bank robbery and jailbreak and any manner of other vile occurrences?

Again I stood there mute for too long.

"It is quite all right, Michael. We do not wish to pry."

"It isn't that, sir, it's just . . ." I did not know how to answer.

Princess Zarah chose that moment to step down from the wagon. She had changed, of course, into her normal clothing, a state which I both approved and quite frankly did not. I preferred that the men of this town not see her in the costume she affected while on stage. But I myself liked it more than a little.

"I'm glad you will be staying with us, Michael," she said with a most charming smile. I gathered she'd been eavesdropping from within the wagon before she emerged. "I feel much safer when you are with us, you know."

I felt a sense of power and purpose welling up in my shoulders and at the back of my neck, and I felt that I stood taller and was stronger than I'd been only moments before. If anyone should approach the wagon in the night . . . well, I'd not be responsible for whatever might happen, that's all.

But, gracious, to think that Princess Zarah looked to *me* for protection.

"So," the professor announced cheerfully. "That matter is settled, eh? Michael, welcome to our little troupe."

He offered his hand, and I shook it with due and solemn care.

Princess Zarah offered hers as well, and I touched her fingertips with both a thrill and a disappointment. A buss on the cheek would have been even better, you see.

Am I giving an impression here that I had been smitten with the princess's charms?

Good!

Because I was.

Hopelessly so, of course, for a beauty such as she, and one of such high station, would have no interest in an ordinary fellow like myself. And anyway I had an obligation to my family that could not be ignored. I was not free to consider my own desires nor even needs. I would not be until that scoundrel leprechaun was brought to bay and Uncle Edward's money recovered.

But—yes—I was both hopelessly and helplessly stricken with—by—this most desirable of all women.

Chapter Sixteen

The road was little more than a track that the desert dearth of moisture kept from being washed away. It was, however, quite good enough for one to see and to follow, and so we traveled slowly southward from Pleasant Prospect.

Princess Zarah spent most of her time in the shaded— but I have no doubt also hot, airless, and stuffy—interior of the wagon while the professor drove and I sat on the forward edge of the seat trying to determine, or imagine that I could determine, which if any of the hoofprints in the road ahead of us had been laid down by my bay.

This creaking, heavily laden wagon could not cope with the bay when it came to simple traveling speed. But then, Liam O'Day had no way to know that I'd survived the near-certain death he left me to. He could not possibly realize that I was on his trail now.

He might well still be chary of the posse, although then again—it pained me to think this after the genuinely friendly and enjoyable evenings we'd spent together—O'Day could have left me behind and horseless as a deliberate form of bait.

He'd broken me out of jail, true enough, and I took that as a gesture of friendship just as he claimed. It was not something he had to do. He was entirely in the clear so far as the law in Lewis County was concerned. Once that posse captured me the law was perfectly well satisfied that they'd caught their man. And would hang him.

No, there was no selfish reason for Liam to place himself at risk a second time just to free me from that jail cell.

And yet once free, he only betrayed me. Again.

Could it be that he'd had second thoughts in the night and decided it was better to toss me to the posse like a scrap of offal thrown into the path of a hostile dog? I could not rule out that possibility.

His reasoning might well be that with me again in custody, the posse would be satisfied. After all, so far as the people of Lewisville Flats knew, I was the one and the only desperado who'd blown that safe and robbed their bank. My never seen and still-unknown accomplice would be small potatoes to their way of thinking and probably not worth chasing out across the desert. Not when they would already have the principal object of their attention in hand. Namely, me.

My head began to ache from trying to worry it all through.

"Michael."

"Yes, sir?"

"Can you drive?"

"Yes, sir, of course."

"With care? We have glass containers back there, you know. They're fragile if jolted too badly."

I managed to keep a straight face when he said that. But only just. The professor's driving was as ordinary as dirt, and if he were making any serious attempt to drive in a smooth and jolt-free manner, he did it in such a way that I could not detect it.

"I can do my best, sir."

"Good. I'm tired, lad. I believe I should like to lie down for a nap. Let me know if we come to any live water, will you?"

I was a trifle puzzled, because we'd filled both water barrels back in Pleasant Prospect and had an ample supply on hand. Still, if that was what the professor wanted, then of course I would comply. "I will, sir."

"Very good, son. Very good." The professor gently eased back on the lines and brought the grays to an easy halt. There was no grass underfoot for them to lip, but they tossed their heads and swished their tails at imaginary flies and snorted a bit to demonstrate their pleasure with this moment of relaxation.

Professor Burdash lifted the buggy whip out of its socket so he could take a wrap of the lines around the iron socket collar, then replaced the whip where it belonged and with an audible sigh climbed down to the ground.

"Is something wrong?" Princess Zarah called out through the small window.

"Not at all, dear. We're changing places, that is all."

"Who?" It was a question the answer to which I rather wanted to hear myself, actually, but would not have been bold enough to ask, much less suggest.

"You and me, dear. I want to rest for a little while. Are you clothed?" It was just as well that I did not use store-bought teeth or I surely would have lost them onto the rump of the off horse when he said that. Apart from the fact that the idea itself would never have entered my mind, the mental image that the professor's question invoked . . . Well, let me tell you, it was not something that would be easily dismissed. Once in my head, it took root and stubbornly grew there.

"Of course, papa."

"Then come out, dear, and sit up front for a while so I can have use of the day bed." He glanced up at me. "Slide over to the driver's side, Michael, and give her your place."

"Yes, sir." He didn't have to say it twice. Before he could finish giving the instruction, I'd completed the act.

The professor walked stiffly toward the back of the wagon, and soon I felt the ungainly and rather top-heavy box sway as weight inside it shifted. Then I heard the door open and again felt some movement of the wagon as Princess Zarah climbed down and the professor entered.

Lewisville Flats

I heard the door latch click shut and the sound of Princess Zarah's footsteps on the hard, caliche surface of the desert floor.

My heart began to race as she approached the driving box to join me.

Chapter Seventeen

Princess Zarah seemed—as I suppose princesses naturally do—calm and composed and serene. I, on the other hand, was a sweating, blushing, tongue-tied wreck.

My problem started when she reached up to me for assistance getting into the driving box. That was perfectly ordinary, of course, and I hadn't really thought anything about it.

Until I took her hand.

The touch of her hand . . . to say that it unnerved me would be a monumental understatement.

I came quite completely apart.

Sure, it was only her hand I was touching. But the sensation I felt went far beyond the normal and reached into places—thoughts and feelings and imaginings—where I really had no business going.

I thought about the sight of her bare feet and ankles. I was acutely conscious of the gleam and the almost liquid flow of her hair.

And—I couldn't avoid it—I thought back to that moment when I'd lost my balance and accidentally fallen onto her.

Princess Zarah thanked me and smiled quite normally and then she did another extraordinary thing. From somewhere she produced a brush and began using it to brush out her hair. She pulled the ends of her hair over one shoulder, the shoulder nearer to me and so it would have been her left one, and began stroking that dark, gleaming mass with the soft bristles of her brush.

It was . . . I'd never before seen anything so intimate nor so arousing. Even more so than seeing her ankles. I tried not to look. Honestly I did. But she was right there at my side, so close I was overwhelmed with the slightly smoky scent of her. And, well, I just couldn't *not* look. Surreptitiously, of course. Out of the corner of my eye and without turning my head. But I looked. Oh, my gracious, I should say that I did.

After a few moments Princess Zarah turned to me, smiling again, her hands still occupied with brush and hair, and she said, "Michael."

"Yes?" It sounded more a croak than a word, but at least I did manage to get it out.

"Papa and I are settled. You can drive on now."

What can I say? I'd forgotten.

Chapter Eighteen

The second day after leaving Pleasant Prospect the track wound precariously down an escarpment to a broad flat with a river running through it and a handful of weathered buildings on the far, or easternmost, bank. The scarcity of trees along the flow suggested the stream could lose its manners when swollen by the spring melt, but there was plenty of crackwillow and other small brush.

"Ah," the professor exclaimed when he saw what it was that we approached, "this would be the mighty Colorado."

It didn't look all that mighty to me. But as we came closer I could see that the ground here had been swept by moving water in a swath that extended for some hundreds of yards before we reached the riverbank. I judged that this must have happened not more than a month or so gone. I was willing to concede that the Colorado, if this indeed be she, could talk back and become quarrelsome when the mood came upon her.

Someone had gone to considerable trouble here to place a set of thick hemp cables across the full width of the river. These seemed to be anchored somehow into the ground itself.

The professor brought us to the river's edge a few feet downstream from the cables. There he stopped and pointed to a signal flag placed upright in a hollow cairn of rocks. "Climb down if you please, Michael, and hand me the flag."

I did as he asked, glancing toward the back of the wagon in the hope Princess Zarah would step outside now that we were stopped, but she did not. Probably she'd peeked through her window and saw that we would be moving again soon, so there was no point in getting out now. The professor, I thought, should take daytime naps more often.

The professor stood in the box and in slow, broad gestures waved the white flag back and forth.

Over on the other side of the river someone came out of the largest of the buildings and stepped out onto the water. At least that is what it appeared he was doing when seen from so far away. What he actually did, of course, was to get onto the long, flat barge that served as a ferry.

The river current, which was swifter than I'd first thought and inconceivably powerful, bore the ferry to the middle of the river. Only there did the ferryman have to overcome the force of the water with a windlass.

As he drew nearer I could see that the topmost and thicker of the cables carried the weight of the barge while the smaller, more easily manipulated was wound onto the windlass. At the other end of the ferry a similar cable-and-windlass arrangement was available for use on the return journey.

The ferryman beached his ugly craft and nodded curtly to the professor, then gave a calculating look to the team and wagon. "Two harses," he said. "Waggin. Two o' you. Thirty cent."

"May I offer you a dollar instead, my good sir?"

The ferryman blinked and grunted, "Whazzat?"

The professor smiled. And repeated his question.

"Hell, yes. I'd take yer dollar."

"Very good, sir. Now, if you would be so kind . . ."

The professor made short work of driving onto the ferry. The ferryman laid planks to bridge the small gap between riverbank and ferry bottom, and the horses trotted aboard as slick as you please. It was obvious to me that neither the professor nor his grays were new to this business of ferrying.

Again the river provided half the effort, then the windlass dragged the weight of boat and cargo alike upstream from the bellied-out center of the support cable. It looked complicated at first glance but actually wasn't. I'd not ever seen a ferry before and enjoyed my view of this one.

On the other side I could see that the buildings too were built onto what looked like small versions of the ferry barge, and they too were anchored into the ground by stout cable.

"Excuse me, sir, but . . . why is your house tied down like that?"

The ferryman snorted. "Comes the flood, son, it's either build me an ark like that Noah fella had or do sum'pin like this 'ere. So come th' spring raise ever' year I tie ever'thin down good an' go over yander a ways to set an' wait for 'er to git back inside th' banks."

I shook my head in true amazement. But the ferryman didn't seem to find anything remotely out of the ordinary in it.

The ferryman put out his planks again and the professor drove us off the barge. He reached down and pulled a fresh bottle of his Belladonna Balm from the bag he always kept close to hand.

I shuddered, thinking we were in for an argument now sure as fire because I could see plainly what was coming.

Sure enough, the professor offered the dollar's worth of elixir to the ferryman in payment for services already rendered.

What I had not expected was that the ferryman accepted the bottle without demur. If anything he seemed rather pleased. "This's really worth a dollar, is it?"

"And a bargain at the price, if I do say so, sir."

"What is it, then?"

The professor told him. In glowing detail, giving the gentleman as complete a spiel as if he were addressing an entire community of potential cash buyers.

The ferryman heard him out, then uncorked the bottle,

gave the contents a careful sniff and then a small, hesitant taste. He gazed toward the heavens in silent contemplation, smacked his lips rather loudly, and then broke into a grinning cackle. "I like it," he declared. "Like it fine. Wouldn't have another on ye, would'ee?"

The professor laughed and handed the man a second bottle.

The ferryman actually reached into his pocket for coins to buy this second bottle, but the professor waved the offer away. "Enjoy it in good health, friend."

The ferryman grinned some more and bobbed his head. When the professor took up his lines and prepared the team to move along again, the ferryman gave him a wink and a nod. "Case ye're wonderin', mister, you didn' put nothin' over on me. I've knowed all 'long 'bout th' passenger ye never tol' me 'bout."

He and the professor both roared with laughter. I thought it was kind of funny too, but . . . how did the ferryman know about Princess Zarah contained inside the wagon there? I never have figured that out.

Chapter Nineteen

At the ferry site the track we'd been following joined with another, much better-traveled road that ran roughly southeast. On the Nevada side—for we were now into Arizona, according to my limited understanding—the larger road went pretty much due west. But over here on the east side of the Colorado River there was only the one road. Which the professor chose to ignore.

To my considerable surprise, instead of following the ruts of the well-marked public road he took the wagon straight south along the riverbank, driving across the desert scrub, weaving constantly left and right to avoid obstacles yet maintaining contact with the river at all times.

I began to be concerned. When we left Pleasant Prospect the professor professed—sorry, but it was inevitable that I'd want to say that at least once—to have no route planned ahead, yet now he acted like he knew exactly where he was going and how best to get there. My concern, of course, stemmed from the fact that Liam O'Day and Uncle Edward's horse money would certainly have followed the road. I'd been content so long as we were on Liam's trail, but I fretted some about this divergence.

Still, my choices were either to stay with the professor—and Princess Zarah—in the wagon or to get down and walk.

Things hadn't turned out all that well the last time I chose to walk across the desert. I stayed with the wagon.

"Ah! Here, I think. Dear?" the professor asked loudly. I was reasonably sure he was not speaking to me.

"It looks good, papa." Princess Zarah was peering out of the window immediately behind my left shoulder and could survey the terrain ahead quite as easily as either of us. I hadn't realized she was so close.

The professor turned the grays toward the river where a flat, sandy finger of land poked out into the river with a backwater eddy downstream from it. I gathered that it was this sort of feature they wanted and that he intended to stop here even though the hour was still fairly early.

He drove us close and stopped, then swung the grays in a tight arc and backed the wagon very close to the water's edge. "This should do nicely," he declared.

Just what it should do was unclear to me. But the need for a fire was an every-camp occurrence. As soon as the professor wrapped his lines onto the whip socket I knew we would be here for a while, so I scrambled quickly down to the ground and trotted around to the back of the wagon so I could help Princess Zarah out of her rather airless confinement, then set off into the willows to begin collecting the makings for a fire.

Aside from dead, brittle willow withes by the armload, there was plenty of sun-dried driftwood to be found there, bits of this and that trapped in the willows during the spring flooding. Unlike some evenings on the bare desert floor, where wood of any sort was as hard to find as an honest lawyer, Princess Zarah would have as large and cheery a fire as she pleased tonight.

Not that I expected more heat to improve her cooking. But there is something undeniably pleasant about a largish campfire, and I intended to provide one.

Chapter Twenty

"Michael." Oh, her voice was soft and lovely. One small word, but she made it sound like music playing.

"Yes."

"Would you help me, please?" Would I help her. Silly question. I added my armload of driftwood to the pile already created and hurried to the back of the wagon. The grays were nearby, hobbled and turned loose to graze on the wiry grass that had sprung up in the aftermath of the spring flooding. The professor was busy with something at the river's edge. Princess Zarah beckoned me inside the wagon, and I rushed to join her there. Alone with her there. For one fleeting second I thought . . . never mind what I thought.

"Papa needs these." She pointed to two bulky and exceptionally heavy canvas sacks that she'd managed to drag onto the floor in the narrow center aisle space. I had no idea where amid all the cabinets, cubbyholes, and small compartments they'd been stored until now. They clinked and clattered when I picked them up, one in each hand.

"Careful," she said. "They're breakable."

Glass. Bottles of the professor's elixir, I guessed. "Where do you want them?"

"Wherever papa says."

I backed carefully out of the wagon and down the step to safer footing on solid ground, then carried the many bottles out onto the spit of sand to the professor. "Princess Zarah said you want these."

"Oh, yes, yes, my boy, thank you. Just drop them over there, if you please."

I did not take his instruction literally, of course, but eased the sacks down with caution instead.

"Now the keg that's strapped to the off side of the wagon, if you please."

I brought it too. It was bulky but light, being completely empty. That surprised me, for all this time I'd assumed it was another water cask, albeit a smaller one.

"Would you please bring the big pot now, Michael, and my supply of, um, medications."

I trusted Princess Zarah would know which he meant. And so she did. She brought out a small, leather-covered and brass-bound trunk that she handed to me. I carried that while she followed along behind with their largest cooking pot and a skein of cheesecloth wound around a wooden rod.

"And now, Michael, I must swear you to secrecy. I must have your oath or ask you to depart until nightfall. The choice is yours."

Had Princess Zarah offered to accompany me on this brief exile, I would gladly have gone. Until nightfall, and considerably longer if that were required. But as no such suggestion was forthcoming, I said, "I'll not tell a soul, Professor."

"On your honor, Michael?"

"Yes, sir. On my honor. I so swear." I thought I remembered something in my mother's reading about affirming instead of swearing, but I didn't think about that until it was already too late and I'd taken the sworn oath just as the professor asked.

"Very good, then, Michael. Zarah dear. Prepare the cloth, if you please. And Michael, I shall need a bucket of water from the river there. But be careful not to dip too deeply. We want to avoid sediments, you see."

"Yes, sir." I didn't see, particularly, but that didn't matter. If he wanted water free of grit and tadpoles and the like, then that was what I would provide.

By the time I brought the first bucket, Princess Zarah had several folds of cheesecloth formed into a pad that she held over the cooking pot. "Pour the water here, Michael."

Which I did, understanding now that the idea was to filter the water and remove any solid particles that might be suspended in the river water.

Two buckets were enough to nearly fill the pot. Princess Zarah stepped aside and Professor Burdash took over, opening his medicine trunk and taking out first a carton of this and then a bottle of that.

He opened an apothecary jar of white powder, moistened the tip of his little finger, and touched it to the powder, which he then quite inexplicably proceeded to rub onto his upper teeth or gums. Whatever the purpose of this, the result apparently satisfied him, for he grunted and used a teaspoon to measure out two careful spoonfuls of the powder. These he dropped into the pot.

There followed small pinches of five more—I counted—powdered or crystalline substances, added one by one. One of them I would almost have sworn was nothing more than ordinary ink powder of a purple-black hue, the same item any schoolboy might use to prepare his inks for a writing assignment. Another looked like common vermilion. The professor measured each with care.

"Excellent," he declared when those half-dozen ingredients were in place. He used a fresh-cut willow switch to stir the powders into the water. "Ready now the next batch."

This first pot full of . . . whatever this was . . . was poured into the keg and the entire procedure was repeated. I got the impression that the professor was accustomed to dealing with these particular quantities; otherwise he might have simply made his concoction directly in the keg rather than going through the slower process of doing it a potful at a time.

The one thing that he did measure out and consign straight to the keg was grain alcohol, added in the ratio of roughly one quart per two-bucket potful of the base mixture. Everything else was done one pot at a time.

Not that I was questioning or criticizing. Merely observing.

"Now," he said after a fourth batch was in the keg. Which would probably have held half a dozen more. "Please be so good as to build us a fire, Michael."

"Yes, sir." I made short work of that. While I did so, Princess Zarah refilled the pot, the professor holding the cheesecloth filter for her while she brought and poured the water. I was tempted to leave off the task I'd been given and rush to help her with this unladylike task. But she and the professor had been managing the entire thing by themselves until now. I kept to the chore that was mine and soon had a fire blazing nicely.

Princess Zarah arranged stones to serve as andirons, and I set the pot atop them so the water could heat.

When it began to steam but was not yet to a boil, she brought out the final ingredient. Horehound candies. Half a gallon or so of horehound candies went into the pot to be stirred until they were melted and reduced to a liquid state.

The professor smiled when finally he poured the dissolved licorice and molasses candy into the keg along with the other ingredients and stirred it all together.

Finally, while the mixture was still warm, he used a dipper to taste of it himself, then offered a bit to Princess Zarah and finally to me.

Professor Burdash's Belladonna Balm, it was. Newly born.

"Do you have the funnel, dear?"

Princess Zarah snapped her fingers and trotted off to the wagon, returning a moment later with a tin funnel that had a very small lower end and a generously large upper one.

We began then, the three of us, filling the bottles that were in those two sacks I'd carried out earlier. I brought a bottle out and held it while the professor used funnel and dipper to actually fill the bottle. Then each went to the prin-

Frank Roderus

cess, who fitted the corks and packed each bottle into a pair of crates that were nearly empty to start with but quite full by the time we were done.

"We don't have enough labels for all of these," the professor grumbled as the last bottles were being secured. "Remind me to have more printed, dear."

"Yes, papa. The first chance we get."

Ink powder. Vermilion. Candy. Alcohol, of course. Lord knows what the other ingredients were. I had no idea what the total cost of all this would be. But I suspected the professor's profits were . . . ample would not be too strong a statement, I believe. Ample.

I carried the new supply of elixir back to the wagon while Princess Zarah began preparing our evening meal, for by then the sun was nearing the horizon and dusk would soon be upon us.

Chapter Twenty-one

"All right, Michael. Which way do we go from here?"

The question surprised me. Breakfast was done and we were ready to roll again, but I'd assumed the professor had his own plans. True to his word, though, he was allowing me to choose, and for that I was grateful to him all over again. As if I weren't already filled to overflowing with both thankfulness and obligation.

I stood there beside the wagon for a moment, trying to work out how to answer him without arousing suspicion. I guess that small hesitation was too much. Or, more likely, the professor already understood something of my situation even if—Lord, I would certainly hope—not quite all.

"Would you like to make some, shall we say, discreet inquiries of the ferryboat man before you select which road we shall follow, my boy?" Both he and Princess Zarah were smiling.

I had to laugh, then said, "No, sir, for people have been known to lie. Hoofprints don't."

"Ah. Very well, then. We shall return to the junction and give you a moment to seek out what you need."

"Thank you, sir."

I helped Princess Zarah into the wagon and made sure the door latch was securely set, then joined the professor on the driving box and he drove us back to the ferry station. The ferryman was sitting outside the front door of his floatable house, chair tilted back against the wall and hat tipped over his eyes. Either he hadn't been dozing or he was a light sleeper, for he stood and stretched immediately upon our return.

"Good morning, folks. Care to cross back over?"

"No, no, only asking for directions," the professor responded.

"That one's north," the ferryman said with a twinkle in his eye and a tiny twitch at the corners of his mouth.

The professor laughed. And nudged me with his elbow. I took his meaning and jumped down to the ground, where I began ambling about in what I hoped would look like an aimless manner.

Behind me I could hear the professor and the ferryman chatting.

Liam would have been through here two, three, perhaps as much as four days ago, depending on how hard he was riding. Not very hard, I guessed, as Liam O'Day didn't seem to undertake much of anything with great vigor. Well, nothing short of eluding the law. And even when it came to that it would have profited him to be considerably more diligent in his efforts, else I might not have been in my current pickle.

Between that and the fact that there was very little traffic through here—we hadn't yet seen a single other wagon, nor so much as a solitary horseman on either road—I was hopeful that the bay's hoofprints might still be found.

On the way down I'd had more than enough opportunity to examine the prints laid down before us, and I was fairly sure I could identify the bay's from their size and rough shape. Some distinctive feature about them would have been most welcome, but unfortunately there simply were none and one hoofprint looks pretty much like another, especially on this hard ground where prints are left poorly if at all.

Besides, I've read some of the dime novels that seem to be teaching the advanced arts of tracking to folks who don't know any better. Don't believe all that garbage. Barring a fresh snowfall, it's darn near impossible to track an animal for any distance more than a couple rods. And even with snow on the ground, a person can become mighty confused mighty fast once the prints get mingled together with others.

No, sir, don't believe all that nonsense. Not a lick of it. White men can't track worth a darn, and neither can Indians. Dogs can smell tracks. Horses can too, except you can't train them to be useful about it, or at least I've never heard of anybody who could. But even Natty Bumpo couldn't track worth sour apples.

That posse member named Dan who tracked Liam and wound up with me instead? That sort of thing comes from working out the man who's being tracked, not any actual hoofprints. Working out where the quarry will be heading and following it there. That's tracking, as pretty much any cowhand can explain, for he'll have had plenty of practice at it when trying to scout out some spooky old cow who doesn't want her birthing place found.

That said . . . I found about half of a hoofprint on the south-leading track that I thought just might belong to the bay and nothing on the broader and better-traveled east-west road that looked likely.

I returned to the wagon, where the professor was in the middle of a commercial transaction.

It seemed the ferryman liked Professor Burdash's Belladonna Balm so much that he was paying cash money for another couple bottles.

Chapter Twenty-two

San Pablo City was the name of the town we came to. I don't know that I would've called it a city, exactly, but I will admit that it was bigger and better established than I expected.

I had always kind of understood that Arizona was raw and new and not much settled until these past few years, most of it coming in the form of expansion following the War Between the States. Apparently, the folks in San Pablo City didn't know about that, for there were a good many buildings, adobe most of them, that looked like they'd been around for generations.

The churches in particular, and there were several of them, looked positively ancient. Left over from the old Spanish and Mexican days, I guessed. And some of the businesses and houses looked almost as old.

Seeing the adobe buildings I'd more or less expected from reading and magazine or newspaper woodcuts depicting Southwest scenes. What amazed me was seeing the outdoor ovens that 'most every house seemed to have beside or behind it. And some of them right out in the front yards, too.

These were also made of adobe bricks, but they were laid up to form fat, inverted cones, the wide circle at the bottom and then tapering down to a smaller size at the top. The whole thing looked kind of like a great big beehive.

They were put outdoors, I guessed, to avoid having the heat from cooking inside the house. And it sure wasn't like the folks who used these things would have to worry about being caught out in the rain while they were fixing their suppers. Dry as this country was, it looked like they'd get rain once or maybe two times in each new generation's lifetime.

It was amazing that anything could grow or prosper here, and I had no idea what these folks did for their livelihood. Well, that isn't quite true. A lot of them must have raised sheep, because signs on several of the businesses offered to buy wool. Apart from that, though . . . well, maybe there wasn't anything apart from that. After all, what the heck would I know about making a living in this country? I was from the north of Nevada, where it only looks barren; it's actually very good graze for those of us who know how to handle it. Could be the same down here, if different in the particulars of exactly how a man coped.

Anyway, San Pablo City was a fairly large and seemingly prosperous place, and certainly a chops-licking, lips-smacking, hands-clenching prospect for the professor. When he saw what we were coming to, he sat up straighter on the seat and looked positively eager.

Once more we did our slow prance from one end of the town to the other, the grays practically dancing. Once more Princess Zarah stayed completely out of sight inside the wagon.

Setting up went smoother this time, for now I knew what needed to be done and was able to anticipate most of the professor's requirements. I got the stage set up, and the professor distributed his horehound candies, and by the middle of the afternoon we were established, so that all we had to do was wait for evening, when the townspeople would be coming in accordance with the news already being spread by the children.

Once everything was in readiness, I secured the professor's permission to go for a little stroll around San Pablo City.

And he, dear man, granted approval without asking any potentially embarrassing questions.

With any kind of luck at all . . .

Chapter Twenty-three

I walked every back alley and peered into every barn, shed, or enclosure from one end of San Pablo City to the next. There was no sign of my bay. Disappointed? More than a little. Still, I did not want to give up, for if he was not here now that did not mean he hadn't been here ahead of me. I headed for the nearest saloon, where there was the sound of a tinpanny piano, for Liam O'Day did dearly love his music.

"Funny-looking little fellow with red hair and a big grin? Sure, I'd be hard-pressed to forget him. Likes his cards, that one does." The bartender seemed a nice fellow, and if I'd had any cash on me I would have been pleased to buy a drink from him. As it was, the best I could offer were a smile and a pleasant demeanor.

"Have you seen him lately?" I asked.

"As recent as an hour ago or thereabouts," the barman said. My heart began to race. "We all heard that snake oil salesman's rig go past, and the boys at the bar all went out to see what the commotion was. Hugh was with them then, but I don't believe he came back inside after that wagon went by."

"Hugh?" I asked.

The bartender gave me a rather odd look. "Your Irish friend. His name is Hugh, right? Or maybe we're talking about two different people." From the suspicion that lay thick as ice on a pond in January, I knew his thoughts were not that we had two people in mind here but that I didn't know Liam's name and was up to something. And of the two of us, of course, it was Liam that he felt he knew, not me.

I shrugged and laughed just a little. "I expect I may've heard his right name in the past, but I don't believe I've ever used it. We've always called him by his nickname."

"And that would be?" The barman still sounded suspicious. But maybe a little less so.

"Slick," I said without missing a beat. "We always called him Slick."

The barman relaxed. "I can see how that would fit him." And then he gave me a bit of a test just to make sure he shouldn't sic the dogs on me or something. "What a great singing voice Hugh has, though, wouldn't you agree?"

"Mister," I said, "it could be we're talking about two different Irishmen after all, for my friend Slick has a voice that'll shatter glass and put a permanent fright into young calves. Ruin them for life so they won't ever again come near to a human if they've ever been exposed to Slick's singing. Why, we had to forbid him from singing even when he was on nightherd, lest he start a stampede. We'd just get him to telling stories to the cows instead, and they'd settle right down and hang on every word he spoke. Darnedest thing you ever did see."

I doubted Liam O'Day was ever closer to a cow than sitting down to eat a beefsteak, but the barman wouldn't know that and cows and cattle are about all I know well enough to speak of.

The bartender laughed. "I was just pulling your leg, friend. That's Hugh, all right. He can spin a yarn, but don't let him start in to singing. Say, d'you want a beer?"

I shook my head. "No, sir, for I haven't the wherewithal. That, well, that's one of the reasons I wanted to find Slick.

See if I could bum a dollar off him until I get paid."

"Tell you what," the now-friendly fellow offered, "I'll go ahead and pour one for you. I can collect from Hugh later."

My heartbeat lifted from a slow trot to a belly-down gallop once again. "You expect he'll be in again soon?"

"This evening. I'm sure he has plans to play some poker again tonight."

Oh my, I thought. After the professor's show maybe? There wasn't anything could keep me away.

Or so I believed at that moment.

I had my beer courtesy of Liam O'Day. Or Hugh. Or whatever his name might prove to really be. Then went back to see if the professor needed anything done while I was waiting for the sun to go down and things to start happening.

About halfway down the street, though, there were two things that struck me, and I didn't like either one of them.

The first was that I hadn't found the bay. Not anywhere in town. I was pretty well convinced I'd looked every place where a horse might be kept, and while there were a fair number of bays among the horses here, mine was not one of them. I was sure of that. Could Liam have sold the bay or swapped him? With Liam, almost anything was possible. And if the bay had been disposed of, what about my saddle and Uncle Edward's horse-buying money?

Lordy, I hoped he hadn't gone and traded that off for a bottle of whiskey or a stake in a poker game.

The other thing, and perhaps even more disturbing, was that I was becoming a liar.

Back there at that saloon I hadn't blinked an eye when the bartender tried to pin me into a corner, just stood there and lied through my teeth and smiled at him while I did it. Me, who'd been raised to be honest and decent and clean. I was becoming about as much of a liar as Liam O'Day.

I was ashamed of myself for that. Or anyway, recognized that I ought to be ashamed, which is almost the same thing. The whole truth was closer to a feeling of satisfaction that I'd been able to handle that situation without making my troubles any the worse.

But now that I thought about it, not only was I a felon and a fugitive, I was a liar too.

It was just a darn good thing the family didn't know about this low state I'd fallen to.

Chapter Twenty-four

I would have to admit that I felt a certain sense of excitement that had nothing to do with Liam O'Day nor with Uncle Edward's horse money. This had to do with Princess Zarah, who continued to keep herself hidden inside the wagon.

The sun dipped low and the crowd began to gather, and as dusk overtook us I went around to the front of the wagon to fetch the matches and light the lamps that I'd earlier bolted to the front of the stage.

Naturally enough, once the lamps were afire and the reflectors adjusted, I stayed right there where I was at the fore. This time, though, the reason was not so much that I might be needed—I would not be, for the professor and Princess Zarah had their show well in hand—but because not only did Princess Zarah perform barefooted and with her ankles exposed, sometimes when she was doing that dance thing the hem of her skirts swayed and lifted so that a person might also catch a glimpse of shapely calf.

And if a person was going to do that, well, I wanted the person in question to be me.

I swear that girl got prettier to me each and every day. Tall, lean, more than a little angular if you got down to cases. But . . . I'm trying to come up with a word here that will explain and yet not be disrespectful, for that is no part of my intended purpose . . . saucy. Yes, I think that would cover it nicely. She had a saucy quality to her that I'd never seen before, not in any woman.

Oh, she was something, Princess Zarah was.

And so of all the folks gathered there that evening I was the most eager among them, for I alone knew what the latter part of the performance would be.

I stood there hogging my stage-side place while Professor Burdash went through his spiel telling folks about the mysterious Orient and far Siam and Borneo and all those unlikely places.

I listened with impatience and wished he would jump right to the good part when Princess Zarah came out, but of course he had to go through each little bit of his buildup so when the time came the people would be primed and ready to drag out cash for the purchase of the wondrous elixir.

Finally, finally, and none too dang soon, let me tell you, the professor made his apologies and slipped inside the wagon, leaving the stage—and my slightly feverish attention—open to Princess Zarah and her exotic charms.

From within I heard the start of the hand organ music.

The handle on the door latch turned.

And the sound of a sharp explosion was heard from some distant part of San Pablo City.

Heads turned, naturally. Even mine. It was that unexpected.

I could see, faint against the evening sky, a thin plume of white smoke lifting into the heavens.

"It's the bank," someone yelled.

"Somebody's robbing the bank," a huskier voice added.

In an eyeblink the menfolk of San Pablo City turned on their heels and began racing madly off toward the smoke and the bank and whatever mischief was afoot down there.

Just that quickly, the professor was left with only women

and children for a buying audience, and those were not the folks he expected to sell to.

I shot a quick glance over my shoulder. Princess Zarah was there on the stage, barefoot and beautiful in the lights. She bore an expression of dismay as she peered down the street after the men, who were by then half a block away and running hard.

My eyes met hers for a fleeting instant, then I too turned and began a race toward the bank.

For unlike everyone else present, I had a very good idea of what had just happened down at that end of town.

Chapter Twenty-five

Oh my, but there was excitement afoot. And sure enough, it was just as I expected. We all got down there to find the windows shattered on one side of the bank building and the door standing open. Not blown open, mind, just left that way by whoever had blown the safe.

And the safe had sure enough been blown open, as the whole town soon learned.

I wasn't among those front-runners who got inside the bank. I'd started behind most of them, and by the time I got there the bank lobby was jam-packed with excited men, each of them trying to tell all the others what happened even though none of them as yet knew what did happen. It was a noisy mess.

Since I couldn't get inside—and wasn't sure I'd have wanted to even if there was room, what with all the nervous gun-waving that was going on in there—I joined a bunch who were standing in the alley that ran along the west side of the building. That was where all the windows were gone. The windows on the east side and along the front were intact.

From this alley we could peer inside. Had to be careful not to slip on the pieces of broken glass that littered the ground here and crunched underfoot, but it was probably easier to see the inside of the bank from here than it would've been from inside the bank, because from the alley window we could see behind the teller counter. Most of those who were inside the bank would be able to see only the backs of whoever pushed his way in before them.

Once they got some lamps lighted and the town marshal dispersed some of the crowd that had gotten into the teller's cage behind the counter, we in the alley had a fine view indeed.

The smoke had dissipated by then, thank goodness, and nothing seemed to be on fire, so I guessed the smoke we'd first seen came from the explosion. I reached that conclusion because there was a sharply acrid scent hanging heavy in the air but none of the usual smell left by a fire.

There was a huge safe set against the back wall. It stood, I would say, a good five, five and a half feet tall and about three and a half to four feet wide and was made of solid, thick, heavy metal. Steel or maybe iron. I couldn't tell about that.

What I could see plain as plain could be was that the safe door, stout and impregnable though it must have looked to begin with, was peeled back as neatly as you would peel the skin off a potato.

The town marshal, whose name I did not know but whose badge of authority was displayed prominently on his vest, investigated the damage and with a look of disgust said, "Nitro. Our thieves used nitro. See here where they drilled?" He pointed. I couldn't see a thing from back where I was, but I was willing to accept the marshal's judgment, as he seemed to know what he was doing.

"They drilled here and here and over here. Poured the charge in and packed it with . . . ," he scraped one side of the shattered door with a thumbnail and held it to his face to sniff and then to taste the substance he'd found there, ". . . mud or clay. Used that to caulk the job. Then touched her off. You can see the result." He shook his head and added, "They used too much nitro. Way more than was necessary."

The marshal called for a lamp and had somebody hold it for him so he could get a better look inside the safe. "It looks to me like they left all the coins. Hard to tell what they might've gotten away with. Herman? I want you and Edgardo to give me an accounting of what's missing. Work through the night if you have to."

From that I deduced that the banker and his chief assistant were among those who'd gained entrance into the no longer crowded teller area. I had no idea which ones they were, of course. Small though the area was, there were probably a dozen men still inside the teller cage.

The marshal turned to face those who were observing all this from the lobby. "Get your horses and your guns, boys. We'll ride out in thirty minutes. I want every man to carry rations enough for five days and water enough for two. And no liquor, dammit. This is gonna be a posse, not a party. Now get cracking, boys. It's the Boyd gang we're after, and we don't want to lose them."

The Boyd gang? Lordy, but that made my blood run cold. The marshal must have received telegraphic notices from Lewisville Flats describing Liam's crimes there but attributing them to me.

Again.

Would that faithless little leprechaun *never* stop bedeviling me?

Chapter Twenty-six

"Pssst!"

I was about halfway back to the wagon, having left the crowd and the excitement behind, when the hiss reached me from the very dark mouth of an alley. I was one of the very first to have walked away, the marshal's plea for posse members notwithstanding, but then none of them was wanted for a large and still-growing sequence of crimes. I figured it wouldn't be a bad idea to get myself out of sight just in case a description had been sent out in that wire the marshal must have received. Now . . .

"Pssst!"

I stopped in the street. But did not approach the alley. After all, I'd heard stories about the way city folks will treat country boys who are not onto their wicked ways. And while I might be wanted as a felon, I was not one and knew very little about felonious ways. If I walked blindly into that alley I might well find myself set upon and . . . well, whoever it was couldn't rob me, now that I thought about it. I hadn't any money to take, nor anything else of value. I shrugged, figuratively if not literally, and edged a little closer to the alley. "Who is it? What do you want?"

"Not so loud, Boyd me boyo, not so loud if ye please."

"Liam!" I blurted. Rather loudly. "What the . . ." I hurried into the alley.

"Hush, lad. I've some advice for ye."

"Yes, and I've some words for you as well, damn you for a faithless monkey. Why did you have to—"

"Will y' hush for half a minute an' listen t' yer auld pal for a mo'?"

"Pal? Did you say pal? As in friend? As in buddy? As in dear companion? Oh, that is rich, Liam. That is truly rich. Here you've gotten me charged with *another* crime, and—"

"Another? Why e'er would they do that?" Liam sounded genuinely puzzled.

"They're blaming this bank job on the Boyd Gang," I retorted.

Liam's response was laughter. "Oh, boyo. Ye're right as rain. 'Tis a rich turn indeed, old son. Innocent as any lamb ye be, an' all my crimes are laid t' yer doorstep." He laughed again.

"The posse is forming now to go after you," I told him. "Give me the money you took. I'll . . . I'll try to square this mess for you. Somehow." I had less than no idea how that task might be accomplished, but I was willing to try.

"Boyd old son, ye're not thinkin' very well, are ye. Do you show up carryin' a poke o' these folks' cash money they're nae gonna thank ye, they're gonna hang ye' from the flagpole. Or whatever else 'ld do, since there seem t' be no trees hereabout. Nay, lad, that idear 'd not be a good 'un."

"You can't keep that money, Liam. It isn't yours."

Which of course brought another outburst of laughter from Liam, who was more than a little impaired when it came to an understanding of personal property rights.

"Boyd, lad, I know what I'm doin' here. While the posse dashes hither an' yon and gets themselves all sweaty an' tired an' worked up, I intend t' relax m'self in the arms o' a charmin' lass. But imagine my surprise, old son, when I chanced t' see you arrive in this town. I'd thought ye safely home by now, boyo. It grieves me t' know that ye're not."

"I intend to . . ." I clamped my mouth tight shut. I could not exactly come right out and tell him that I was trying to recover Uncle Edward's gold, could I? I mean, that would not be inviting the fox into the henhouse, that would be the same as killing and plucking the chickens for him too.

"Hush, lad, an' listen, for I've a wee bit of advice here. Dinna mention me name, lad, nor tell 'em what I look like, an' we both shall be gettin' out o' this, as free as birds. Just keep shut an' go on about yer affairs an' all will come well. Trust me." He laughed again.

Trust him. Right! That was a laughable suggestion indeed.

"I'm sorry, Liam, but I cannot let you get away with this. I have to . . . Liam? *Liam?*"

It seemed I was speaking to an empty alley. I could sense that I was alone there.

And a moment later I could sense as well that someone was standing behind me. I turned to see two of the townspeople staring into the darkness of the alley. I gathered that my leprechaun had sprinkled some of his magic dust once again—or whatever it was he did in such circumstances— and was gone now as silently as a moving shadow. How he'd known those men were coming . . . Well, it didn't matter, I supposed. But it unnerved me a little just the same.

"Howdy," I said.

"Are you all right, mister?"

"Sure." I stepped back out to the street, fiddling with the buttons at my fly as if just finishing buttoning up again.

"We heard voices," one of them said.

"Reciting lines from a play," I told them with not a heartbeat's hesitation. And this time felt not a whit of guilt from the lie.

"Of course." The nearer of the men smiled. "Say, I recognize you now. You're the fella that helps out with that traveling perfesser, aren't you?"

"Yes," I told him. "Yes, I am."

"Sure hope he sticks around and puts his show on again. I got a quick look at that girl. Does she . . . I mean . . . just

181

what-all *does* she do, friend?" He winked and chuckled and dug an elbow into his buddy's ribs.

Me, I went cold. I had a strong impulse to see just how close to the back of his head I could move his nose. But I didn't need the trouble that sort of behavior might bring, not with *two* posses out looking for the notorious Boyd Gang.

I said nothing, but apparently my expression, whatever it may have been, and perhaps the tension in my shoulders and posture made the message as clear as words could have done.

The two townspeople clammed up, and the one who'd just spoken took a stumbling half-step backward.

He stammered out something that I believe was intended to be an apology, then turned on his heels and began walking quickly, very quickly, back in the direction he'd just come, back toward the bank and the safety of numbers that he might find there.

His friend hesitated just long enough to show me that unlike his buddy this one wasn't afraid—although he was, as I could plainly see—then he turned and hurried to join his pal.

I glanced into the alley once again. But Liam was long gone from there.

Disgusted, I headed back to the wagon.

Where were the bay horse and my saddle and Uncle Edward's money? I'd had my chance to ask Liam but hadn't done it, thinking there was time enough to talk and not having quite worked out how I could pose those questions without raising suspicion.

Damn it. Damn it all, anyway!

Chapter Twenty-seven

"No harm has been done," the professor declared after breakfast the following morning. "The people will come again tonight. We shall simply remain here until tomorrow." He smiled. "We need to replenish our supplies anyway. We will simply keep the wagon and stage where they are for the day and get our shopping done in the meantime.

"Zarah dear, I want you to draw up a list of staple foods and groceries we need. Michael can go with you to help carry them. I shall find a pharmacologist and secure our coca powder and alcohol. We seem to be running low on both of those, and it may be some time before we see another town this large. I am sure this San Pablo place will have a proper apothecary."

"Should I put horehound on my list, papa? I don't think we have many left."

"Please do. And whatever else you think." He smiled and reached into his pocket for a purse, from which he extracted a twenty-dollar double eagle that he handed to Princess Zarah. "Michael," he said.

"Yes, sir?' "

"This is for you." He gave me a ten-dollar piece.

"Do we need grain again, sir?"

The professor snapped his fingers. "Of course. Thank you for reminding me." He brought out another coin and said, "Use this for the grain."

"Yes, sir, but . . ." I looked at the eagle that remained in my hand. "What is this for?"

"Why, it is for all the help you've been. Surely you don't expect me to accept your labor and not offer suitable reward."

"Sir, you and Princess Zarah saved my life. I owe you more than a little labor."

The professor waved the words away with a sweep of his hand. "Nonsense. And we'll hear no more of that, Michael. We . . . yes, gentlemen?" He spoke to someone who stood behind me. I hadn't been aware of anyone's approach, but when I turned I could see the town marshal there and several armed townspeople with him.

It was still early in the day, and I had to wonder what had become of the marshal's bold intentions for his posse. The men were instructed to take five days' rations with them, as I recalled.

Of course, in order to remain on the trail of the desperate Boyd Gang a posse would require a trail to remain upon. And I knew for a certain fact that there was no trail to be followed. Liam remained in San Pablo City along with the rest of us. Probably the posse determined the futility of the chase shortly after daybreak this morning. That would account for the marshal's presence now.

The marshal nodded toward me but spoke to the professor. "We've come to ask about your man here," he said. "I've received a description of the man who robbed our bank, sir. The telegraph came through overnight. This fellow fits the description mighty well."

"Really?" the professor asked. "That does sound serious, doesn't it?" He eyed me closely for a moment, and my heart stopped beating during that time.

I was uncomfortably aware that three of the marshal's men had moved to stand close behind me, and I was reminded anew of the harsh treatment I'd had at the hands of that other posse back in Nevada.

Even so, I was determined that I would not meekly submit to them. If they wanted to take me in, they first would have to take me down. And that might not prove so easy a task this time, as lately I'd lost my innocent belief in the fairness of the law and of lawmen.

"Would it help you to know, Sheriff, that my assistant Michael Stewart has been traveling with us for the past . . . what is it now, Michael?—three and a half, going on four years. And last night when that explosion occurred, Michael was standing here beside the stage in full view of half the population of San Pablo."

Now all of that was a powerful whopper. About as fine a lie as I could have concocted myself. The professor looked the marshal squarely in the eyes and reeled off those untruths without apparent qualm.

"That's right, Sheriff," Princess Zarah put in, prompting the gents to snatch off their hats and openly give her the attention they'd already been giving out of the corners of their eyes. I gathered that they were quite as smitten as I, and never mind that Zarah stood a good five or six inches taller than they. "Michael has been with us for years." Her smile would've charmed the malice out of a rattlesnake's heart. "And I can assure you he has been up to no mischief in the evenings." She batted her eyes and stepped closer to link her elbow with mine. "None that any of you gentlemen would be interested in, anyway."

My cheeks became warm as ovens, and I'm sure they were red as a fresh apple. I certainly took her meaning, and I am sure the marshal and his men did also.

Zarah winked at me and laughed. She didn't seem to care in the slightest what these gentlemen might think.

It would be true and then some to say that I'd never met a woman like this before. And hadn't ever expected to, either. Princess Zarah fair took my breath away.

Her effect on the marshal was equally strong. The marshal bowed just as polite as ever you could hope to see, then said to the professor, "Please accept our apologies, sir. We intended no disrespect."

"Certainly none is taken, sheriff. You are but doing your jobs. And doing them well, if I might add. I hope you will accept our best wishes for a successful capture of the brigand who made off with your bank's receipts, sir."

"Thank you, sir. Thank you very much. Now, if you would excuse us." The marshal bobbed his head toward the professor in a gesture of respect and again toward me, although perhaps with a somewhat different sort of respect. Envy would be more like it. Then he bowed again to the lady. "By your leave, ma'am?"

Princess Zarah held her chin high. "It is 'miss' if you please, sir."

"Yes, ma'am. I mean . . . yes, miss. Good day, ma . . . iss."

"Good day, sir."

My goodness, but Princess Zarah was clearly the person in control of this little gathering. She and the professor were a cool and collected pair indeed.

And this was the second time that they'd saved my life. I had no doubts whatsoever about the truth of that statement.

Chapter Twenty-eight

We were pretty well stocked up with rice and potatoes and like that, to the point that my arms were aching and I set the packages down whenever I saw the chance. Princess Zarah was moving from store to store, humming and smiling and bargaining the merchants down to prices that would've scandalized their wives. If their wives had been around. I noted this in particular because in the one establishment where the proprietor's wife was within earshot Princess Zarah picked and chose just as careful as always. But she didn't try to beat the fellow down on his prices.

"Could I make a suggestion, miss?" I asked after about the fourth place we'd shopped in.

"Of course, Michael."

"Well, I was thinking . . . that is, I'm not much of a cook . . . but I do know how to put together some trail food. Would it be all right . . . would you mind if I was to pick out some things and cook them up for us sometimes. I'd pay for them out of the money your daddy gave me, mind you. I'm not trying to work a cheat on you."

"Why, Michael." I'd once thought she was an angel? The

187

radiance of her smile confirmed that now. "How very kind of you. Of course you shall pick out anything you want. But I'll not hear of you spending your pay on our food."

"Oh, miss, I already owe you and your daddy more than I could repay in half a dozen lifetimes."

Lordy, but this was one almighty handsome young woman.

I began working up my nerve right there and then to speak for her. After what she'd allowed the marshal and his men to believe, well, I didn't think my hope was too awfully misplaced.

On the walk back to the wagon, I decided. I'd work out my speech while we shopped and then spring it on her when there was just the two of us walking back to the wagon.

"What would you like to cook, Michael?"

"Hoecakes, I think, and flannel cakes too. A jerky stew—that's one of my best recipes—and of course beans and bacon. Beans and bacon are what you might call traditional."

"All right. Pick out whatever you wish."

So I did. Couple slabs of smoked bacon. Big old sack of spotted beans. Some chili peppers. The red; those little green ones are too much for my stomach. Molasses, of course. She already had me packing flour and a couple pecks of cornmeal, so we were all right for those.

I looked around and considered what all of this would weigh and who would have to carry it and decided we had enough for this experiment. After all, they might not like my cooking, and I never like to see good food go to waste.

"Is that it?" she asked once I had it all to the counter.

"Yes, that's plenty."

"All right, then, Michael. But can we make two trips to take it all back to papa's wagon, please? All of this seems terribly heavy."

That sounded like a splendid idea to me too, for after all, if the two of us walked back and forth together for a second time, that would put me alone in her company just that much longer.

In my excitement at that prospect I grabbed up so much

stuff that I was in danger of getting it all transported in one trip. And I sure didn't want that.

"Ready when you are, miss."

She smiled and nodded a pleasant good-day to the proprietor and off we went, she walking, me sweating. And not from the weight of the groceries, either.

Chapter Twenty-nine

"Ma'am. Miss. Could I ask you something . . . well, something personal?"

"Of course, Michael. We are friends, are we not? You may ask me anything."

We were near about back to the wagon with our second and final load of food, and if I didn't ask her now I likely never would. I got up my courage as best I was able and willed my heart to quit trying to run away out of my mouth.

"Miss Zarah . . . what you said to those men this morning . . . you know what I mean. And I been thinking . . . I mean, I know I'm not such-a-much to look at. But I got a good heart. Everybody tells me that. And if I have troubles with the law right now, well, I can explain that. It isn't so serious as you'd think once I can get a good lawyer who will keep me from hanging."

"Michael. Gracious. You sound like quite the desperado." She laughed and laid her fingers on my arm. When she did that I felt the same sort of charge you get in wintertime when you shuffle your feet across wool carpet and then touch something metal.

"I have to tell you, Michael, that I admire a man who is a fiery individual. Did you kill someone? How many? Tell me about this, Michael. I love it."

"I didn't kill anybody, and it isn't exciting as you might think. Just a bunch of mistakes and wrong assumptions. Anyway, that's not what I want to talk to you about." I stopped then. Right in the middle of the main street of San Pablo City. I didn't care who saw us talking together in private like that.

"What I'm wanting to say, princess . . . Say, can I call you Zarah?"

She shook her head. "No, but you may call me by my real name, Michael. My name is Sarah. Papa changed it for, shall we say, professional purposes."

"Sarah. I like that. Sarah Burdash."

"No, Michael, my last name is not papa's."

"No?"

"It is Collins. Plain little Sarah Collins from Warfordsburg, Pennsylvania."

"Oh."

"As for the question you want to ask me but haven't . . . please do not, Michael. I do like you *ever* so much. I truly do. But . . . Michael, you've been inside our wagon."

"Yes, of course. Couple times."

"Tell me, Michael." Her expression became gentle, and again she touched my arm, just above the wrist. Funny, but this time I didn't feel any electrified charge from it. "How many beds do we have built into the back of our wagon, Michael?"

"Why, just the one along the right side, of course. It . . . oh. Oh, dear Jesus God," I blurted. For the second time that day I felt heat rise in my face.

"Michael, when I call the professor 'papa' it is a game we like to play. He is not my father. He is my teacher. My mentor. The best and truest friend I ever hope to have. And, Michael. He is my lover. As I am his. And I shall belong to him until death takes me away from him."

I turned my head away. I could not at that moment bear to look into those sultry eyes.

191

Lord, I'd been blind. I felt a queasiness deep in my stomach and wanted to throw up.

"You don't . . . I'm sorry, princess. I mean Sarah. I am so sorry. I hope I haven't . . . embarrassed you."

She gently squeezed my wrist, and then, there in front of the entire town, she rose onto her tiptoes—she hadn't far to go to manage it—and gave me a dear and friendly kiss on the cheek.

"May I tell you something, Michael?"

"Of course. Anything."

"If things were different, if Baltzer were not already in my life, I would have been honored to receive your attentions, for you are a fine man, Michael Stewart." She grinned and brought a lighter tone to the conversation by adding, "You will make some lucky woman a fine catch, Michael." She giggled. "If they don't hang you first."

She turned and hustled back to the wagon, and I had to hurry to catch up.

Chapter Thirty

"Which direction shall we take this morning, Michael?"

I couldn't believe the professor and Sarah intended to have me continue in their company. Surely Sarah had told the professor about my stupid indiscretion yesterday, but neither of them mentioned it, neither by word nor by implication.

"I . . ." I was at a loss for words.

"Take your time, son. We are well supplied now. And we took in more than ninety dollars in cash money last night and some mining company scrip that may be worth something."

"I think . . . I think . . ." I paused and wiped my eyes and blew my nose and looked out over the rumps of the thick-bodied grays.

I hadn't a clue where Liam might have chosen to go from here. And had no idea if he was still on the bay. If he'd switched to a different horse and ambled away to make his escape once the San Pablo City posse returned without coming to grips with the desperate Boyd Gang . . . I just didn't know.

"South," I heard myself saying in a firm voice. "We should travel the road to the south from here, sir." After all, where would a fleeing bank robber choose to go except south? To Old Mexico.

"Very well, Michael. South it shall be." The professor gave me a smile and reached beneath the seat for a bottle of his elixir. We both had a small nip to launch the day, then the professor shook out his lines and took up contact with the grays' snaffle bits.

The wagon lurched forward, and we were on our way.

Three

Chapter One

It wasn't the same traveling with the professor and Sarah after that. They were nice to me. They always had been. But . . . I didn't look at either of them quite the same any longer. The little things I'd thought of as being normal father-daughter affections . . . well, they weren't. At all. And now . . . seeing those small mannerisms, sleeping beneath the wagon at night.

That, I think, was the worst of it. Lying there a few feet away and wondering . . .

I gave up sleeping underneath the wagon and began laying out my blanket beside the fire instead. I'm sure Sarah and the professor noticed the change, but neither of them mentioned it.

We drove south along the poorly defined track another three days and came to a tiny burg named Solitaire. It wasn't much, but it was all there was, and the professor made his usual preparations for the show, setting things up with my assistance and having Sarah in her role as Princess Zarah come dancing out onto the stage to the shock and delight of this almost exclusively adult male audience, Solitaire being somewhat lacking when it came to children or decent women.

It was funny, but I no longer saw Sarah quite the same way I had before. Her performance seemed—I hate to say this, but it is true—it seemed almost lewd to me now. Tarty, the women in my family might have put it.

Before I'd been as entranced as any man in the audience who was seeing her for the first time.

Now her displays of flesh, and barely concealed intimation of more than was actually seen, struck me as bordering on the indecent.

Now I began to think of the dismay and disapproval that would surely have resulted had I brought Sarah home to my family.

Oh, neither my mother nor my sisters nor very many of the cousins would actually have *said* anything unkind. Not where Sarah would overhear, and certainly not so that I would ever have known.

But the whispers and speculations would have flown in private, and none of them would ever have been happy had Sarah been my choice for the future.

I was better off to have avoided all of that.

I should have been quite happy with this discovery.

Funny, but . . . I was not.

If anything, I was quite thoroughly miserable now.

Still, the show went on and the men clamored for the privilege of buying the professor's products. They were thinking, I believe, that once the selling was ended the dancing would resume, and the trade was brisk.

The professor had taken in ninety-some dollars back in San Pablo City. Solitaire was probably a tenth the population, but I know for a fact that the professor's take here was in excess of sixty dollars. And nearly all of that was profit.

He spent a few cents for the bottle, which was the most expensive item required. A quarter cent or so for the label and as much again for the cork. And a few cents more for the actual ingredients, the primary one being nothing but river water filtered through cheesecloth. Call it a dime at the utmost, and probably the costs totaled closer to a nickel.

For a product that sold for a dollar. Not bad business, actually. If you wanted to look at it that way.

Had I not owed Sarah and the professor the debt of a life, I think I would have felt quite harshly toward them for gulling purchasers as they did. And for the fleshly promise implied in Sarah's unseemly public display of her scantily clad self on a lighted stage.

Still, there was nothing I could say or do. I had to find Liam O'Day and recover—somehow—Uncle Edward's horse-buying money.

I *had* to.

And if I wanted to do that, well, what choice did I have but to put my own thoughts and desires aside. I needed to bite my tongue and bide my time and do that which needed to be done.

Having reached this inescapable conclusion, I was prepared to travel with Professor Burdash and Zarah the princess of . . . wherever she was supposed to be princess of . . . until Hell froze over, if that was what was required of me.

Imagine my surprise, then, to find myself fired from this unpleasant but necessary employment with neither cause nor warning.

Chapter Two

"I'm sorry, Michael. Or should I call you Robert? But the fact is that I am growing weary of Princess Zarah making moon eyes at you."

The Robert thing confused me for a moment. I'd almost forgotten that the professor knew that name, thanks to the town marshal back in San Pablo City. The Boyd Gang and all that.

As for his comment, Sarah was *not* making eyes at me. Nor did I any longer want her to. That was but an excuse for the professor's actions, not a valid reason.

"I admit that your assistance with the stage and other necessities requiring," he sniffed and lifted his chin so that he could peer down his nose at me, "brute strength has been something of a relief to me. And keeping Princess Zarah out of sight is a positive aspect of your presence in our little troupe. But the plain fact is that you are becoming a disruptive influence. I've decided it will be better for us all if you go your own way from this point."

I couldn't help it. I looked around. It was shortly after dawn and the wagon was loaded, the team hitched, and everything in readiness for Professor Burdash's traveling medicine show to pull out of Solitaire.

Where, apparently, I was to remain.

Solitaire was, to put it bluntly, quite solitary. There was little here except a handful of adobe or daub-and-wattle shanties and a pen where a few pitifully ragged-looking sheep were kept.

And this was where the professor chose to fire me. Thank you very much.

I looked around. Swallowed. Told myself quite sternly that I would *not* grumble nor fuss nor utter a single word of complaint. Not one. If the man wanted me to leave his company, well, it was his company and his entitlement. Damn him.

"I gather from our friends to the north that the reason you are without funds, Robert, is because of a breakout from jail. I shall not comment about that, but I quite frankly do not feel responsible for your current, um, predicament."

"No, sir, you are not," I said, as it was the simple truth.

"I shall, of course, grant you severance pay." He hesitated, then added, "Princess Zarah asked me to do this. I do not feel it is necessarily owed to you, but out of the kindness of her heart she has asked me to offer it."

I got the impression that he wanted me to refuse the small cloth poke that he now produced.

Refusal, of course, would be the gentlemanly thing to do, as the professor was making it entirely clear that giving it was not his desire.

"Thank you," I said instead. And held my hand out. I was in no position to be gentlemanly at this moment. Not with two posses searching for the desperate Boyd Gang. Of which I seemed to be the leader.

The professor handed the poke to me and harrumphed a little as if to underscore his disapproval.

"Good day, Michael. Or Robert. Whoever you are today." He climbed onto the driving box of his medicine wagon and took up the reins.

Sarah—and come to think of it, why did the professor now insist on referring to her as Princess Zarah still, even though he knew perfectly good and well that I was acquainted with her true name—remained out of sight inside the wagon.

She did not wave or say good-bye.

The professor put the grays in motion, and the wagon rolled on, turning away from the southward path we'd been following since leaving San Pablo City and taking a westward course instead.

Toward California, that would be.

As for myself, I was still intent on pursuing Liam O'Day and Uncle Edward's missing money.

All I needed to do now was find a way to accomplish this despite the fact that I was afoot and friendless in a sunbaked Arizona village and with the law back in Nevada desirous of hanging me.

Still, I'd been in worse straits before this. Much worse, come to think of it. That cheered me no end, albeit in a left-handed sort of way.

At least now my life was not being threatened. My belly was full. And I had a purse in my hand containing . . . I had no idea how much.

But I was not penniless. I was not hungry.

And I was not in jail awaiting sentencing and hanging.

Yes, sir, now that I thought about it, I wasn't so bad off after all.

I sent one last look in the direction of the dust cloud raised so thick by the iron tires that I could no longer see Professor Burdash's wagon, then walked into the center of Solitaire to make a few discreet inquiries and then see what form of transportation I might be able to arrange for myself.

Chapter Three

I am not complaining. At least that is not my intention. But the professor left me with rather little in the way of cash that I could use to equip myself for the further pursuit of Liam O'Day and Uncle Edward's money.

In retrospect, I suppose the truth is that I was treated fairly by Professor Burdash. Or so I have been assured by several people with whom I have discussed the matter. I was with the medicine show working as their roustabout for a matter of several weeks, and he'd paid me ten dollars back in San Pablo City. I still had most of that after repaying that nice bartender for the beer he'd given me on tick.

And now the professor had given me another ten, this time in the smallest of small change collected here in Solitaire. When still inside the pouch it looked and sounded like considerably more than was the fact, and I could not help but wonder if he'd deliberately given me the pennies and tupennies and three-cent pieces so as to make Sarah think he was more generous than this. Now that she was irretrievably gone, you see, I found that I was consoling myself with the professor's parting comments and convinc-

203

ing myself that if I'd stayed close by, the princess—Sarah, that is—might have had a change of mind regarding me.

Not that a girl so saucy as Sarah would have been an appropriate companion to take home to mother. But, oh my, she was certainly exotic and enticing and—to be blunt about it—arousing in ways I'd never known before this journey.

It seemed that I was experiencing perhaps more than the family intended when they sent me off to face the world on their behalf.

And not only in my reactions to Sarah nor even anything having to do with the novelty, if one cares to think of it in that manner, of being a felon with the specter of the hangman close by. This thing about the money, for instance.

For all my life until this journey I'd had no real concern with nor in truth much interest in money. Money in anything more than the smallest of amounts was something that served the family, not the individual family member. If I wanted for anything, all I had to do was mention it. To my mother, my father, perhaps to my uncle or to Aunt Ethel.

Whatever was desired would be sent for the next time a catalog order was placed. For pocket money, each of us might be given a small amount whenever we went to town. And even that was done seldom. There was hardly a business establishment in Kyne Springs where the Bar X Bar did not maintain an account and where any member of the Little family could buy on credit.

Well, there was one place where cash would have been required. But I'd never visited that particular, uh, establishment. And if any of my cousins did, I was unaware of it.

All of that, however, was then. And this was now. In a dusty little Arizona shantytown called Solitaire and not the comfortable surroundings of Kyne Springs, Nevada.

I had in my possession just short of twenty dollars now and a great many needs that had to be met with it.

I needed food, water, and transportation. I had to, absolutely *had* to, resume my pursuit of that miserable little leprechaun Liam O'Day. Yet there I stood, with nothing in the way of possessions but the clothes I wore and the hat

Liam had left for me. Everything else I once owned was gone now, either with Liam, back at home on the Bar X Bar, or locked away in a drawer somewhere in the Lewis County courthouse.

The pittance that I now held would have to go a very long way indeed. I adjusted the set of the little Irishman's hat and set off in search of a mercantile so I could do my shopping in anticipation of what I hoped would be a fruitful journey to the south.

Chapter Four

This was embarrassing. Or anyway, would have been if there'd been anybody around that I knew. Being among total strangers who I'd never see again made it possible although not really comfortable to hold my head up in public.

The thing was, after buying a bath—I smelled so bad there just wasn't any choice about that and no surface water anywhere near where I could sluice away some of the dirt and dust—and a few items of food and a rubberized canvas water bag and a pocketknife and a blanket and the remnants of a bale of light rope and some matches and a magnifying glass and a folding saw—you know, the usual things a man has to have if he wants to get along without civilized amenities—I hadn't money enough left over to pay for a horse.

If there'd been any horses for sale in Solitaire. Which there weren't, probably because of the high cost of keeping one in the middle of a desert.

Nor a saddle.

Nor a mule.

Nor much of anything else except. . . . What I'm getting at here is that I ended up with a gray-muzzled old creature

that the fellow selling it admitted was more than twenty
years old and so was probably a heckuva lot older than that.
Into its thirties, could be.

I felt kind of sorry for the poor old thing. But I reasoned
that carrying my few possessions was going to be a lot easier
on it than hauling a hundred fifty or so pounds of water
from a distant spring into town, which is what the owner
had been using it for up until now.

Anyway, the only form of transportation I could find—
and that was for my stuff and not for me, as there was no
way it could've handled my weight in addition to everything
else; Lordy I do hate to admit to this—it was a burro.

Yes, one of those fuzzy-eared, dewy-eyed, rat-tailed, tiny
wee little dang burros. I mean . . . I've owned dogs that
were bigger than that scruffy, scabby, patchy-coated burro
was. Seemed bigger, anyway. This thing . . . it came up to
about my waist. It was that little. If ever I had climbed on
and tried to ride it, it would've collapsed under my weight.
And if the silly creature's legs did manage to walk a few
steps with me on its back, the toes of my boots would've
dragged furrows in the dirt.

My humiliation, I knew, was now complete. It had been
bad enough to face felony charges and a hanging. Now I
had to go about in public with a burro for company. And
one that was probably older than I was, at that.

If I hadn't absolutely needed to travel on after Liam
O'Day, I would have . . . I don't know what I would have
done. Gone home, of course, although I have no idea how
Walking, I suppose.

Which of course was what I would have to do now in
order to continue south. I had no other choice except that.

And since I couldn't pack food and water and stuff on
my own back and expect to survive down here, well, the
burro it would have to be.

"He is a good burro, *señor*," the previous owner assured
me. "You see he has the cross of the Savior here on his
body." He pointed out the dark stripe down the little animal's spine and matching stripes that ran from its withers
down the front legs on either side to form what did indeed

look like a cross. "All burros have this," the gentleman told me. "It is their reward, *señor,* for it was one of their kind that carried the Savior on its back, no?" He smiled. "This burro's name, he is called St. John the Baptist, *señor.*"

"Comes to that name when you call him, does he?" I asked, although not serious of course.

The gentleman only laughed. I glanced into his pen at the three other, younger and presumably stronger burros he still owned. Would have sold one of them to me, too, except that I couldn't dicker him down to a price that I could've afforded after buying my other things. But then, he knew I had to have something to carry my gear. He could see that much just looking at the things I'd been toting in my arms when I walked up to his place. He knew he had me over a barrel and would be able to get my last cent out of me for whatever animal he wanted shut of.

Turned out to be St. John the Baptist. Which was not, perhaps, a bargain. But then, what other choice did I have? I could buy the burro or I could pick my stuff up and start walking again.

So I paid over everything I had with me and accepted the scrap of rope that was looped around St. John the Baptist's neck.

This was not my finest moment.

I took a look at the sun. It was still short of noon and I had plenty of time to make a start after Liam O'Day.

I figured I would probably curse that Irishman every step of the way between here and Mexico.

But the only way to get there was to take that first step and then a whole lot more after it.

There wasn't a pack saddle nor frame that came with the burro, and the seller probably thought he would be able to scrape me in a barter for one, but this time I had the advantage of him, being no stranger to packing horses and mules at home. I'd been doing that pretty much all my life and had no difficulty putting everything securely in place on the burro's back.

With that I gave the gentleman a cheery adieu—I might be embarrassed here, but darned if I would show *him* that—and set off afoot into the desert, me and my burro alone under the burning sun.

Chapter Five

Any new outfit takes some getting used to, I suppose, and all the more so for this departure from what I was accustomed to.

By nightfall my feet hurt. Of course. I couldn't think of any remedy for that short of finding a horse and saddle wandering loose in the countryside. Fat chance of that, of course.

But there was something I could and would do about St. John the Baptist. When I pulled his pack that evening, I could see that the rope I was using to substitute for cinches and a proper pack saddle were galling his skin behind his forelegs and a little bit also, if less so, under his belly.

I couldn't allow that, firstly because if I ruined the burro I would have nothing but my own broad shoulders to carry my stuff, but also, I admit it, because it just isn't in me to see any living thing suffer.

I didn't have any balm or salve to put on him to help the little fellow heal, so I made do. First I watered him, using my hat for his trough. A sip for him and a sip for me, and that would do for each of us. I didn't know how far the next water might be and did not intend to be caught out again without any.

After that I built a small fire and cooked a bit of bacon, which would serve two purposes. The first was to provide my supper, the second to create a little grease, which I captured on a rock and used to rub into St. John the Baptist's gall marks as an unguent of sorts.

Finally, I got out my brand-new pocketknife and my brand-new blanket and proceeded, with no small amount of difficulty, to cut thin strips of blue woolen cloth off the blanket.

With those to pad the ropes where they wound underneath the burro, I figured St. John the Baptist should be safe from further abrasion. The remaining chunk of blanket, about half of what was there to start with, I could wrap around my torso at night to sleep in—there was enough left for that, although not enough to cover my legs too—and then during the day use as a saddle blanket placed underneath the burlap bags I was using to pack my things in.

That solved St. John the Baptist's problems. It also demonstrated a rather critical need to sharpen that knife.

I knew when I bought the thing that it was cheap. But I'd expected it would at least have an edge on it. After all, what is the point of anybody carrying a dull knife? So whyever would anybody sell a knife that had no edge? It didn't make much sense to me.

For whatever reason, though, that knife was about as sharp as Liam O'Day was honest, and something had to be done about it. About both of those things, come to think of it, but I was not yet in a position to discuss honesty with that no-account leprechaun while I could do something about the dull knife blade.

Not having had the foresight to add a whetstone to my purchases, I found a suitably rough chunk of stone on the desert floor and set about honing the edge on that. It took most of the evening, but after going through three different rocks selected for their grittiness and finishing up on the side of my boot, I eventually had an edge that I wasn't ashamed to carry. Fortunately, I hadn't anything better to do with my time and so counted the evening a success.

Now, if I could just think of something that would take away the aching in my feet from all this unaccustomed walking . . .

Chapter Six

It was the afternoon, I think, of the fifth day that St. John the Baptist and I reached paradise.

Not a town of that name, you understand, but the place itself. And if it wasn't actually paradise, then it was certainly close enough to it for my purposes.

I say here that I "think" this was the fifth day because in truth I am not entirely sure. When you are walking across an empty, burning desert one moment is much the same as any other and the days run together like lumps of lead all put into one crucible and allowed to melt into one shimmering, silvery mass.

In any event, fifth day or sixth or whatever, the wagon track we were following took an unexpected and most unusual turn toward the east while a much smaller path continued straight south.

I could see no obvious reason for this until I traveled a little farther along and realized that to the south of the road a half mile or so there was a deep depression in the earth. Not a canyon exactly but a wide swale or valley.

I detoured back toward the path that I'd shunned and as

I approached the lip of what turned out to be an escarpment that defined the north side of this valley.

And down in the bottom I could see green grass and mature trees and cattle grazing on either side of a thin stream. Off to my right, toward the west, a small waterfall fed a pool at the base of the cliff, the overflow from this tank coursing out into the valley to join the flow of live water there. The sound of the falling water was like tiny bells in the stillness of the desert heat, and St. John the Baptist pricked his fuzzy ears and curled his lip a few times before letting out one of those rasping, buzz saw brays for which the desert canaries are famous. The burro could hear and probably smell the water, and he seemed as eager for it as I was myself.

I could see now why the wagon road did not continue here. The face of the escarpment was much too severe to permit a road wide enough for a wagon to safely travel, but time and animals—wildlife or livestock or both—had carved out a steep, narrow path.

There was no question but that the burro and I would descend into this oasis of grass and water. We still had several gallons remaining in the water bag, but that fluid, precious though it was, was stale and flat and tasted of the sun-scorched rubber coating that waterproofed the canvas. This water, and some recuperation in the shade of a real tree, would be just the thing to restore body and soul.

I knew better than to attempt to lead St. John the Baptist down such a difficult path. When he neared water he was very apt to bolt forward, and, taking a cautionary look at the rocks below, I did not want to be knocked aside in the burro's zeal to reach bottom.

I looped the lead rope over the little animal's neck and gave him a tap on the rump to send him down ahead, then gratefully followed into the green and much cooler depths of the valley.

Paradise indeed, I thought, when I knelt at the pool beside St. John the Baptist and plunged my head and shoulders deep into the chilly water.

Chapter Seven

Paradise? Oh, God! I'd descended into purgatory. Now there was but one long step left to take. Straight down to the end of a hangman's noose.

They'd caught me.

I woke—again—to the sight of men with drawn guns surrounding me.

There were—I looked behind me and all about—five of them. I did not see the sheriff nor the tracker. Don, was he? Dan? Something like that.

There were no familiar faces in this bunch. But their intent was certainly clear enough. They had rifles and revolvers. No shotguns, though. Oddly enough, the lack of a shotgun to cut me apart made me feel somewhat better; I can't imagine why.

"Did I tell you, boys?" one of them said. "Look in the valley, that's what I said, wannit? Go to the water. That's where he'll be. An' so he is." He barked out a short, sharp laugh that I did not find to be particularly amusing. "Go to the water. Ayuh, here he is."

I was still wrapped in my half blanket, but I stirred now so as to sit upright.

"Watch him, watch him," the leader warned, and the rest of them cocked their guns. The leader already had his hammer drawn back. "Easy, mister. Don't make any fast moves if you want to live long enough to hang."

"Now, there's a pleasant prospect," I observed. "I don't own a gun. I just want to sit up now." The statement about not owning a firearm might technically be questionable as to truthfulness. If it was locked away in the Lewis County courthouse, did I still own it? Or did they? I decided not to debate the point at this moment.

"Fine, but do it slow an' easy."

"Do I know you?" one of the other men asked.

I looked at him closely, then shook my head. "I don't remember you, mister."

"You look kinda familiar to me," he said.

I looked at him again, but still with no recognition. On the other hand, they all looked alike to me at the moment, all of them with the beginnings of whiskers from going a number of days between shaves. As I had myself, of course, having shed my beard back in Solitaire when I got that bath. Now I was growing a new one like it or not, since I owned no razor. "No, sorry."

"Your name is Boyd, innit?" the leader asked.

"My name is Michael Stewart," I corrected, that being the name freshest in my mind at the moment. And I certainly would not have wanted to admit to the Bob Boyd name in any event.

The one who'd spoken before snapped his fingers. "Hell, yes," he said. "That's where I seen you. You was with that medicine show, wasn't you?"

"Yes, I was," I told him.

"Lonny, I remember seeing this fella back in San Pablo. The marshal mistook him for Boyd then, and that perfesser fella vouched for him. Said Stewart worked for him a long time. Couple years or thereabouts. The coochie-coochie girl vouched for him too." He looked at me. "Hey, come to think of it, what're you doing here if you work for that perfesser?"

"I left him in Solitaire. His idea, if you must know. He didn't like the way I was getting close to his daughter."

The man from San Pablo rolled his eyes. "Mister, I'd like to get close to that myself. D'you do any good with her?"

I didn't answer that, of course.

"You say she's his daughter? I thought she was some high an' mighty princess from someplace in the Oh-ri-ent."

"She's his daughter," I said. The fact that she wasn't . . . I was not going to shame her before these strangers. "Her name is Sarah. She's a nice girl."

"Nice? Yeah, she looked nice, all right." He made a remarkably lewd remark as an expansion upon that opinion.

And I had had just about enough of posses and guns and threats and ugliness.

One good lunge and I planted a right hand on the shelf of his jaw. The punch had all my considerable weight behind it, and I knocked cold the man who'd just saved me from hanging with his confirmation that I was not Robert Boyd.

The other posse members, thank goodness, were convinced enough at this point that they did not shoot. Nor, for that matter, did they decide to mix it up with me on behalf of their now-unconscious friend. I guess my mixture of fear, indignation, and fury was enough to intimidate the whole damned posse. And if they all damn five of them wanted to take me on, well, I was more than ready for an excuse to put bruises on every dang one of them, one at a time or all of them at once. Right at that moment I was truly that peeved.

After that, however, things calmed down some. They brought cold water from the pool to pour onto the San Pablo man and bring him around, and they broke out the makings of a breakfast that they shared with me once it was done.

My day, I would say, had been off to a rather bad beginning, but fortunately things took an upswing after that.

Chapter Eight

The second day south of that paradise/purgatory valley I came to the ranch where those cattle must've come from. I knew, of course, there had to be one in the vicinity due to the presence of the livestock, and the path I was following led me to it.

It was a ramshackle, sprawling sort of outfit with one main house that looked like it was added to without rhyme nor reason whenever somebody took a notion to throw a new room into the pile.

The house was made of adobe. And stone. And some daub and wattle. And for all I knew, there might have been some kiln-fired bricks and shiplap cedar wood stuck somewhere inside the mess. This place just kind of rambled every which way, so there was no telling what it might've looked like to begin with nor how long it had been growing there.

The outbuildings were strewn about with the same fine degree of planning that'd been put into the house design. That is to say, they were scattered across the countryside like a child's game of jacks. Just sort of allowed to fall wherever they might.

Set more or less in front of this architectural wonder was a downright magnificent gate with tall posts on either side and a slab of hewn timber above it with the Rocker W brand burned into it. The gate was left open by way of a welcome. Which was just as well, since there was no fence on either side of the gateway. Just those posts and timber and the gate itself. The path ran between the posts and through the gate, so that's the way St. John the Baptist and I went when we approached the place.

"Anybody to home?" I called out as we entered the yard.

Was there anybody home? Lordy, you'd've thought I stomped an anthill when I shouted out like that.

Heads began popping out of doors and windows in every direction. Most of those heads being small and all but one of them topped with jet-black hair. Whoever lived here was a breeder, that was for certain sure.

The most of them were children, I quickly saw. They were what my mother calls stair-steppers. Looked like there'd been a new one come along every year for the past dozen or more, and they all came rushing out to meet me.

Except it turned out it wasn't me they were greeting but St. John the Baptist. They swarmed around him like he was a litter of new puppies, each of the kids wanting to admire him and touch his fur—that burro was, I must say, about the hairiest creature I ever did see—and exclaim over him in what I took to be Spanish.

They also spoke English. Which I discovered when one of them asked, "What's his name, mister?"

So I told them. That brought a squeal of delight out of the little ones and equal, if somewhat quieter, enthusiasm from the older ones.

"St. John the Baptist, St. John the Baptist." It became a singing refrain of sorts, and the children danced around and around the little burro, who did not seem at all to mind the attention he was getting.

"Can we give him something to eat, mister?"

"Sure, go ahead."

A couple of the kids went racing off into the house. They came back half a minute later carrying a basket with what looked like fresh-that-morning biscuits in it. They offered the biscuits to St. John the Baptist, who seemed to enjoy them right well. I would have, too, except they weren't offered to me.

Following close on the heels of the children with the basket was a tall old man with gray hair, bifocal spectacles, and a belly the size of a washtub. He extended a hand when he reached me.

"Robert Weir," he said. "My name is spelled W–E–I–R and pronounced 'Wire,' and if you call me Bob Wire I'll throw you off my place. Otherwise, you're welcome to stay as long as you like."

I laughed and introduced myself. As Michael Stewart again, just in case that posse was still in the neighborhood. I kind of hated to do that, though. Not only was I just plain tired of lying to people, there was something about this man that I liked from the first time I saw him.

He seemed . . . I don't know how to explain this properly, but Robert Weir looked about as contented as any man I've ever met. Happy and cheerful and at peace with the whole wide world.

"Come inside, Michael, and meet Mrs. Weir." He turned and said something in Spanish and two of the older boys jumped to take St. John the Baptist's lead rope from me. "Don't worry, Michael. They will take good care of him."

"I wouldn't have thought otherwise, Mr. Weir."

"Robert. Please call me Robert."

"Yes, sir. Thank you."

We were skirted around to the right of the house and passed through a small gate into a walled garden with what looked like grapevines growing over an arbor that covered about half the flagstone paved courtyard. There were chairs and a table and one of those funny-looking beehive ovens.

A plump—all right, the truth is she went past plump and was just plain fat, round as a doughball and ninety percent of her body weight devoted to her smile—woman with streaks of gray in her otherwise black hair was tending to something in the oven. She left whatever it was and came at a trot with both hands out and that smile preceding her like the reflector lamplight ahead of a locomotive.

I thought she was going to grab my hands to shake. No sir. She grabbed hold of me in a hug instead.

Me. A complete stranger. She hugged me.

I'd never had anything like that happen to me before. Not in my whole life. My *cousins* didn't hug me like that, nor even my own mother, we being a somewhat reserved bunch at home, and it made me feel . . . I don't know. I liked it. I can say that much for sure. It was . . . nice. Warm. Kind of sweet.

I mean, I might have been the bank robber and safe blower that some thought I was, and these folks wouldn't have known any different, and yet as a visitor I was welcomed with a hug.

There wasn't any doubting the sincerity of these folks. No sir, not no way.

"Ma'am," I said, and snatched my hat off just as soon as I could get a hand free to do it. "It's a pleasure to meet you."

Her smile got even bigger—which I would not have thought possible, since it was so wide to begin with—and she began talking to me in Spanish.

"I'm, uh, sorry, ma'am, but I don't have any Spanish."

"Jew," she said.

"No, ma'am, I'm Christian," I said. Which got quite a horselaugh from Robert and Mrs. Weir.

"Jou are welcome here," she said in slow and rather halting English. I gathered that Spanish was the normal tongue in use in this household, although the kids obviously had no trouble with their daddy's native language.

"Thank you, ma'am. Thank you very much."

"Come inside, Michael. You can give me the pleasure of some conversation. We don't see many passersby, and I'm always eager for news from the world outside our happy home."

At that moment, to tell you the truth, I couldn't see why he would care what happened elsewhere. I thought I'd seen paradise back in that valley a few days to the north?

No. What I was seeing here was the truer paradise. A

happy couple with their children around them and no malice toward any man. Now, that was paradise.

I followed Robert into the cool interior of the crazyquilt house.

Chapter Nine

Dinner that evening was a study in chaos. The dining "room" was the long table under the grape arbor. And as big as it was, the table wasn't near long enough to accommodate all those children. Places were laid for Robert and Mrs. Weir and for the ranch foreman, a gent named Carlos Montoya, and for me. The rest of the table was given over to bowls and platters and plates of eatables.

The only time everybody was holding still was when they all gathered together while Robert Weir said grace. In Spanish. But I know that's what he was doing, because he did that thing about crossing his heart before and after he spoke and of course all of them had their heads bowed. And their mouths shut. But that was about the only time that condition prevailed.

Soon as they were turned loose upon the food, the children darted in on the table like hawks stooping onto prey. They'd grab a tortilla—which is a flat cornmeal pancake sort of thing that tastes better than it looks—pile it high with whatever struck their fancy, and be gone again.

They ate in clusters and bunches, perched at various

points around the courtyard. Everybody talking at once. All of them eating and gossiping and laughing, sometimes all three at the same time, or so it seemed.

This was not the sort of thing I was used to, my family being sticklers when it came to table manners and silence unless one of the older folk posed a question.

But I have to tell you that I enjoyed my experience with the Weirs thoroughly. And the food was good too. Spicy and mighty unusual. But tasty once I learned what to expect when I bit into something.

Afterward I tried offering to help clear the table. You would have thought I'd insulted them.

"Don't even think about it," Robert said. "Come along inside. I need to get my daily report from Carlos, then the three of us can relax and have a drink before we crawl in for the night."

"If you don't mind, Robert, I'd like to find out which bunk is mine so I won't be stumbling over any of your vaqueros in the dark."

"Bunk? Nonsense, Michael. You'll sleep in the house with the family. You're a guest, not a hand. Besides, I doubt any of the hands over there has any English. Well, other than a few words suitable for starting a fight." He looked me over and added, "Not that I think any of them would want to try a visitor your size." Then he laughed.

"I don't want to put anybody out."

"You won't. We'll just pick up our strays and pitch them all into a bedroom together. Like worms in a can. They'll love it."

"Really, sir, I can't take anybody's bedroom away from them."

"You already have. The boys brought your things in before supper. And if you want a bath or a shave, feel free. There's no hot water, but we've put the tub in your room and there's soap and a razor there too. I know how it is traveling in this country. You'll feel better if you have your shave and bath."

I didn't know how to thank the man for his hospitality.

Chapter Ten

"Are you sure you won't stay a few days more, Michael?"

"Oh, no sir, I couldn't. I need to catch up with, uh, my friend."

"Of course. I understand. Could I ask a favor of you, Michael?"

"Anything." I meant that, too. I felt like I owed Robert Weir as much, although in a completely different way, as I'd owed to Professor Burdash and Sarah. There was something about this family—I'd never known anyone like them.

They . . . I think the best and simplest explanation is that these people really, and I mean *really*, loved each other. My own family was wonderful. Don't get me wrong about that. And all my life they'd been absolutely everything to me. But there wasn't this . . . closeness . . . there that the Weir kids seemed to find with their parents.

In our family the emphasis was on obligation. And in truth there was a lot of competitiveness involved. Not just between me and my cousins, but among all of us. Older folks, younger generation, all of us. We Littles weren't cold. But we weren't like this Weir bunch, either.

After two days resting here and eating like a hog at the trough, it had already occurred to me that if I'd been one of the kin on this place I wouldn't have hidden my name to try and keep things from getting back to the home folks. I think I would have just hollered for help. And gotten it.

And now Robert wanted a favor? If it was mine to give, it would darn soon be his to own. "Anything," I repeated.

He smiled. "You know, Michael, the children are really quite crazy about that silly burro of yours."

"Yes, sir," I said with a grin. "It would've been hard not to notice." The kids treated St. John the Baptist like he was a new kitten for them to play with. Except one that was big enough for them to crawl onto and ride while somebody led them around the yard. St. John the Baptist seemed to like the attention every bit as much as the children did, too.

"I hate to ask this of you, Michael. But would you consider trading your burro? I would be willing to make you a good deal. I could swap you one of my rough string to replace him. And I have some old saddles lying around that you could have. Riding saddle or a pack rig, whichever you want. Do you think that might be possible?"

I have to admit that I wasn't sure if Robert was trying to trade so the kids could have their pet, or so I would have a horse to ride instead of a burro to walk beside the rest of the way to Mexico. Either way . . .

"Yes, sir. I'd be happy to make that trade."

"Good. Let's walk over to the corral and you can pick out something that looks good to you. I, uh, assume you can handle a greenbroke horse?"

I winked at him. "I expect I'd be willing to try," I said.

And a pretty good little tussle it turned out to be, too. I borrowed a catch rope that was hanging on the gatepost for the purpose and dropped my loop over the neck of a likely-looking bright sorrel that wasn't much for tall but looked like it might be pretty good for stout.

It stood quiet but trembling while I cinched on an old McClellan saddle that Robert produced from a shed somewhere and stood quiet enough while I climbed into the saddle.

Whoo-whee! That little horse could sure rip. I hadn't yet had a chance to set my boots properly into the stirrups when he laid his ears flat, bogged his head, and went to twisting.

There wasn't any horn to grab hold of on the surplus army saddle, so I clamped down hard with my legs, jerked my hat down tight on my head, and let that horse introduce himself.

It was fun, actually. Sure enough woke me up. By the time the horse decided which of us was going to be the boss, I had the taste of blood in my mouth from where I'd bitten my tongue a couple times and more blood running down my chin from the nosebleed he'd gotten started. My head ached, my back hurt, and I was probably three inches shorter than I had been from my spine being compressed by all his stiff-legged jumps.

But I was still on his back, and he wore out a good thirty seconds or so before I would have.

"What do you think, Michael?"

I could only grin. Turned my head and spat so as to clear my mouth and then was able to say, "I like him."

A cheer went up from along the corral rails where all the children and most of the Weir vaqueros were watching.

I nudged the sorrel forward, and he walked polite as you please to the gate, stood quiet with his sides heaving while I opened it and led him out, then continued to stand quiet while I stepped back onto him and rode him around to the front of the barn to where my stuff was piled.

It was mighty good to be on a horse's back again, let me tell you.

Robert had a bill of sale already made out except for a description of the horse in question, and he quickly filled that part out and handed it over to me. "We wouldn't want anyone to think you're a thief," he said with a wink and a laugh.

"No, sir, we surely wouldn't," I agreed just as solemn and serious as I knew how. The exchange made me wonder, though, just what Robert knew, or thought he knew, about this stranger who was passing through on his way to Mexico.

"If you're ever back this way again, Michael . . ."

"Yes, sir, I wouldn't think about riding past without coming by for a meal and a talk."

I was ready to step back onto the sorrel and go. But I couldn't. Not yet. Darned if all those kids didn't come leaping and larruping after me so they could give me hugs around the neck. Mrs. Weir hugged me, too.

I was . . . it was the darnedest thing. Those children barely knew me. Yet they were giving me hugs. The least of them was a big-eyed, black-haired, chubby little girl who couldn't have been more than three, four years old. She put her arms tight around my neck, and I could feel the wet of her kiss on my cheek.

I mounted and rode out of there in a hurry, I don't mind telling you, quick lest I do something completely stupid like get teary-eyed to be leaving these people that I scarcely knew.

Chapter Eleven

Los Palomitos. I guessed that meant something about palm trees, because I saw some there. First time I'd ever seen such a thing, although of course I'd read about them. There must have been a couple dozen of them in this town, and I rode the sorrel horse right up to the first one I saw and just sat there for a minute marveling at the thing.

It was tall and spindly and looked like it needed a haircut, being all shaggy and strange-looking at the top. But at least now I knew what one of those palm leaf things actually looks like. They were like I expected from the pictures, except when there was a breeze they rattled together and made a sound kind of like falling rain. Which in a way was funny, because the country around here looked like the last time it rained in the neighborhood was when Noah was building his ark.

Anyway, I got my fill of looking at the palm trees and then rode onto the main street of the town.

I'd never seen a Mexican town before either, of course. This one was built all of adobe, and pretty much every-thing—buildings, street, and distant views—was all the

229

same color. Dirt. Pale, dry, sun-scorched dirt. A man didn't come here for the scenery.

Still, there was graze available in the desert. I'd learned that over the past five days since I left the Weir place. The sorrel had to work to find his dinner, but he'd always managed.

As for myself, I was down to pennies. Literally. I had exactly nine pennies in my pockets, and if I didn't find Liam O'Day soon I was going to have to look for some sort of work before I could go on, because I'd run out of food two days north of here and my belly was becoming peeved with me for neglecting it so.

I tied the sorrel to a rail that didn't look stout enough to have held St. John the Baptist, but it was all I could see short of tying him to a roof post. And I didn't think the business owners hereabout would appreciate that. Anyway, the sorrel was proving to be a pretty decent pony now that we'd worked out who was in charge. By this time his morning exercise was limited to no more than a dozen or so half-hearted jumps, and I didn't begrudge him that small display of cussedness. A horse that doesn't have any spine generally doesn't have any bottom, either.

The few signs facing the street were written in Spanish, and so far as I was concerned might as well have been written in Greek, for one was the same as the other to me.

My nose took me into a place with lettering over the door that said "Cantina." I didn't know who or what Cantina might be. But there was the familiar scent of beer wafting past the curtain of fly beads over the door, and that was enough to make me think this was the place I was looking for.

"Howdy," I said to the dark-haired, mustachioed gent behind the bar. "Speak English, mister?"

"Got money?" he countered. I guess the dust I was wearing gave me away, for if I'd been heavy in the pockets I probably would have found a bath before a drink.

I grinned at him. "I expect you do at that." I eyed the free lunch spread and pretended to examine the various jugs and bottles on a back shelf before I said, "I'll take a beer, thank you."

He just stood there, looking at me, patient enough but not moving, until I reached deep into my pocket and pulled out my treasure hoard. I counted out five pennies, cupping my hand so he couldn't see what else might be there, and laid them onto the bar. That took me down to four cents, but the beer would slake my thirst and the free lunch would fill my stomach. Five cents seemed a bargain to me.

The barman drew my beer—and I have to admit he was nice enough about it and blew off some of the froth so there was room to fill the mug rim full—and exchanged it for my pennies.

"Mind if I ask you something, mister?"

"You can ask anything you like," he told me. "Whether I answer or not remains to be seen."

I tasted of the beer. The bitterness was crisp on my tongue, and the beverage washed my throat clean of dust. "That's good stuff," I said. "Thanks. I'm down here looking for a friend of mine. Little redheaded Irishman. Looks kind of like a leprechaun." I was hoping this Mexican fellow would know what that was. He sure did speak good English for a Mexican, though, so maybe he would.

"Mister, I think you've been drinking too much already." I gathered that, yes, apparently he did know the word.

"I didn't say he *is* a leprechaun. Just that he looks like one. Sort of." I took another careful swallow of the beer. I wanted it to last until I had a chance to get at that lunch spread. But Liam O'Day came first.

The bartender shrugged. "I haven't seen any little people in here, mister. Nor fairies or other strange creatures. And no Irishmen lately except for Bill Bates, and he's a great huge lump of a man. I don't think anybody would mistake him for a leprechaun."

I shrugged and made as if it wasn't anything of consequence. "Never mind, then. Thanks."

The bartender left me alone then, ignoring the two other

fellows in the place at the time, and left, going out a back door.

I took that as a good omen and began laying waste to the ham and cheese and pickled eggs on that lunch tray.

Chapter Twelve

All right. Maybe it wasn't such a good omen after all. The bartender came back. Through the front door this time. And he wasn't alone. There was a lanky, redheaded fellow with him, but the redhead sure wasn't Liam O'Day. This one was tall and had a shiny badge pinned to his vest.

The bartender went back behind his bar. The redhead came over to stand beside me at the lunch tray.

"Yes?" I asked around a mouthful of cheese and dry cracker. Some flakes of cracker sprayed onto the lawman, but he affected not to notice.

"Would you mind telling me your name, mister?"

"Michael Stewart," I answered. The name had served me well enough in the past.

"I don't suppose you would have anything that would prove that," he said.

"No, I wouldn't. I . . . wait a minute. I do have the bill of sale for my horse. That has my name on it. It's in my bed-roll."

The lawman scowled. And followed right beside me while I went outside and down the block to where I'd left the sorrel. He watched close while I untied the rolled-up blanket behind my cantle and reached inside.

"You can bring out anything you want, bud, but if it's a gun I see in that hand the fault will be your own."

I glanced around to see that he had his own revolver in hand now. It wasn't cocked, but it was aimed in the general vicinity of the small of my back. I can't say that I liked the feeling it gave me to know that.

"I don't own a gun," I told him.

"If you say so." His gun never wavered.

I went on with finding and bringing out the bill of sale Robert Weir had given me. Slowly. Very carefully.

The lawman motioned me away from the horse, and I complied. Only then did he drop his eyes to the paper.

"Bob Weir gave you this?"

"Yes, sir."

"How d'you know Bob?"

"I'd call him a friend," I said. Which was the truth. I couldn't claim we were *old* friends, of course. But that wasn't what the man had asked, was it.

The lawman grunted. Folded the paper and handed it back to me. Better yet, he dropped the revolver into his holster.

"Nathan said you're looking to meet up with a friend here."

"That's right."

"And your name is Michael Stewart."

"Right again," I agreed.

The man looked doubtful. But he said, "I'd suggest you watch yourself while you're in this town."

"I'm not doing anything wrong. Don't expect to, either."

"I hope that's true."

"May I ask you something?"

"Sure," he said.

"How is it that an American would be marshal in a Mexican town?"

"Mexico?" For the first time I saw something other than a hard look in this man's expression. "You think you're in Mexico? Mister, you are in the Territory of Arizona, in the

United States of America, and I am an Arizona Ranger."

"I'll be damned," I said.

"That could well be," the ranger agreed.

I started to turn back into the cantina to where I still had half a beer and about a third of the free lunch layout remaining on that bar, but I was distracted by something I saw—or thought I saw—about two blocks down the street.

I would almost have *sworn* that I saw Liam O'Day standing at the mouth of an alley down there.

By the time I got down to that alley, though, there was no sign of Liam nor anybody else there.

And by the time I got back to the cantina, there was no sign of the rest of my beer either.

"Hey!" I barked.

The bartender, whose name apparently was Nathan, only glowered at me and made no offer to replace what he'd taken off the bar.

I decided, under the circumstances, it probably would be better if I didn't find myself in any trouble right at that moment.

I went off to see if I could find some sort of odd job I could do, else I was going to be mighty hungry again mighty soon.

Chapter Thirteen

Good Lord! This was the prettiest girl I'd ever laid eyes on. Sarah—Princess Zarah if you like—was handsome. But this girl was . . . angelic, almost. Of course, her size would suit her more for Liam O'Day than for Boyd Little, as she was tiny wee. I'll bet she wouldn't tape out to five feet nor weigh anything close to a hundred pounds, but what there was of her was mighty fine.

She had gleaming black hair that hung down below her waist and bright, huge, sparkling black eyes and lips . . . I'd best not get to thinking overmuch about those lips, for they were enough to put a flutter into my stomach and a lump in my throat.

I was about half smitten with her. And all she'd done was open the door in answer to my knocking.

She was standing on the stoop and I was on the ground, and even so she had to tip her head back and look up to look into my eyes. I wanted to reach out and touch her. Just touch her hand, that was all. The impulse was so near to overwhelming that it worried me.

I guess I was acting the fool, standing there mute like that after rapping on the door. But I couldn't help it. My mouth was dry and my hands sweaty, and I could hear my heart-beat thumping loud as a drum inside my ears.

"*Sí?*" she asked. "*Que es?*"

I blinked. Didn't answer whatever it was she'd asked. I doubt I could have answered even if I'd understood the question.

Another voice asked another question, this one from somewhere inside, and the girl turned her head to answer. Oh my, but she had a voice like it had been distilled from the purest honey. When she turned her head her hair flowed like black water. Down here in the southland where girls wore their hair down, I was discovering that long hair had a powerful effect on me that I hadn't known was there.

The girl held up a finger to tell me to wait where I was, then disappeared inside. I could hear voices indoors and then the door frame was filled by a woman who was almost a duplicate of the girl except older and with some streaks of gray in her hair. The two looked enough alike, though, to have been sisters.

"You have Spanish, *señor?*"

"No, ma'am," I said, trying to look past her to the girl.

She laughed a little. "Her name is Juana, and she is my daughter. An' what she says to me just now is that there is a *guapo, muy guapo* Anglo come to our door. She tells me he is," she paused for a moment, and I suppose she was searching for the word, "much . . . I mean very . . . very handsome Yankee man come to call."

I felt a flush. Don't know if it reddened my cheeks, but there was heat in it. Not from embarrassment, though. This was from pleasure. The girl thought I was handsome? Oh my! I didn't think anybody'd ever thought that before. Not ever that I knew about it, anyhow.

The woman stood there. Smiling. Eventually—it could have been a whole minute or more—eventually I realized that she was patiently waiting for me to say something. After all, I had come knocking on their door.

"I, uh, that is to say . . ." I was still trying to peer past her into what I could see now was a kitchen. Very busy. But

then the place was a café around to the street side. I'd come
to the back door after I spotted what looked to me like some
work that needed doing. "I, um, I see there's a lot of wood
out here. Scattered all around, like. I, uh, I thought maybe
you'd like somebody to stack it for you and split the rest of
those chunks over there."

"You look for work, yes?"

"Yes, ma'am." Funny thing, but when I told her that her
expression didn't change and neither did her posture. You
probably know what I mean. A person will talk and stand
and act different with somebody who's their equal, as op-
posed to how they are when they're talking with somebody
they think is beneath them.

My aunt Ethel has never been known to turn a hungry
man from her door. That wouldn't be the Christian thing
in her mind. But she has a way of looking at them that lets
them know they aren't the same to her as respectable folks.
I suppose somewhere deep down I was expecting to be
treated that way here now that I was the one who was down
on his luck and looking to exchange work for a little help.

But it wasn't that way at all. This lady—can I call a Mexican woman a lady? I guess I just did anyway—this lady was
just as welcoming and pleasant now as she'd been to start
with. It was the darnedest thing.

"You are hungry?"

"Not right off. I had something to eat at a free lunch
spread over to the saloon. Excuse me, the cantina. But I
don't have enough money to buy another beer, and tomorrow I'll be hungry. I'd be glad to work for you this evening
and have a meal tomorrow, ma'am."

"You are strong. Big."

"Yes, ma'am."

"You can break apart those log?"

"Yes, ma'am. Easy."

"You work for food."

"Yes, ma'am, if you will."

She smiled again and nodded. "You work, you will eat.
You want to eat now? You are not hunger now?"

"No, ma'am, I'm fine, thank you."

"Is good, *señor*."

"Yes, ma'am, thank you." I bobbed my head and twisted the brim of my hat, which I was still holding in my hands. And I looked past the lady again but couldn't see the girl. Juana. Mighty pretty name, I thought.

I turned and went to see just how much wood I could get split and stacked before nightfall.

Chapter Fourteen

My hands stung where a couple blisters had broken, but that wasn't enough to keep me awake. Even so, I lay there on my half-blanket staring at the stars when I should have been sleeping.

I'd laid my gear out on a slab of hard caliche. It wasn't much for softness, but it beat sleeping on thorns. The sorrel was hobbled and set loose to graze. He hadn't wandered far. I could hear the brittle clatter and soft, ripping sounds as he nosed into clumps of brush to find the few stems of succulent grass that sometimes grew in the shelter offered by the thicker brush. This was a desert horse and seemed content enough with this effort. I'm not sure my good bay, familiar with the dry but much more productive rangeland up north, would have survived nearly so comfortably.

My night thoughts were a strange mixture, jumping back and forth between two subjects, each of which was powerful.

One was Liam O'Day. The more I thought about it, the more positive I was that I'd seen him here in Los Palomitos, standing at the mouth of an alley just a couple blocks from where I'd been talking with that ranger.

My eyes are good, and the figure I saw hadn't been so far away that I should be mistaken about it.

It was O'Day, the miserable little SOB. I was sure of it. Nearly sure.

It couldn't have been imagination or wishful thinking that I spotted him there. Could it?

That was what kept haunting me in the night. Had I really seen him there? Or did I want to see him so badly that I imagined him?

I'd seen him. I believed that most of the time. But I kept coming back again and again to the possibility that what I'd seen was not really Liam O'Day but some . . . I don't know. Maybe that is why people claim to see leprechauns, too. Imagination fueled by the desire to see them.

Maybe Liam O'Day was *becoming* a leprechaun in my mind. A ha'nt. A ghostie. An imagining of the night so strong in influence as to be seen in daylight too.

In other words, maybe I was losing my mind.

Just a little. Oh Lord, only a little if at all, please.

I sighed. And returned to thinking about the other subject that kept pulling at me now.

Juana. So delicate. She was a flower of the desert. Pure and pretty and sweet. The smile. The lips. The legs.

Oh my, the legs. The fashion down here was for girls to wear their skirts with the hems cut calf high.

Up home that would have been scandalous in the most literal sense of the word. Even a woman of the night, one of those that decent folk call soiled doves or other made-up names instead of coming right out and speaking the truth about them. But up home even a hoor—there, I said it— even a hoor would have caused a commotion had she worn so short a skirt out on the public streets. She would be run clean out of town. On a rail if need be. And the gossip would run on for years after.

But here . . . I had to admit that I liked the Mexican style more than a little.

And Juana looked almighty good. Her ankles were small and her calves slim, and she was prettier than a sunrise.

She was working in the kitchen while I was working out

back, and every little once in a while I would make an excuse to step inside so I could ask for something. A drink or a question that didn't really need answering. Any excuse was good enough. Not that I think anybody was fooled anyway. I kind of suspect that both Juana and her mother knew all along.

I went in there, I'd bet, eight or ten times, and Juana was there stirring pots and washing dishes and slicing vegetables and whatnot, and I think she was prettier and her hair glossier and her smiles brighter every time I saw her.

I should have been thinking exclusively about Liam O'Day and that hanging posse and Uncle Edward's horse-buying money and important things like that. But my mind kept coming back to Juana and to the way she looked and the way she smiled and . . . Lordy, but I wished that girl could speak English.

The good thing, of course, was that come morning I would get to see her again. Juana's mother—come to think of it, I didn't know her name nor their family name—insisted on feeding me supper after I worked and told me I was entitled to a breakfast, too.

I was not going to pass up the opportunity, let me tell you. The food was important enough. Seeing Juana again was even better. My only regret was that I'd gotten every chunk split into stove lengths and every split piece stacked tidy and proper. There wouldn't be more work for me to do there come tomorrow. Darn it.

Chapter Fifteen

Tortillas and what they called refried beans, that was breakfast. It tasted better than it sounds. I'd waited until most of the breakfast rush was done before I showed up for my promised meal. I hadn't wanted to take up their time and space when there were paying customers who were entitled to that attention.

Pretty good thing that I'd done that, too, because Juana, looking even prettier today with a bow holding her hair back and a skirt that I think was hemmed even shorter than the one she'd worn yesterday, was busy scrubbing tables while I sat there, the only one in the dining area at the moment. I have to confess that I liked watching her when she bent over to wash the tabletops. I didn't let her see that I was looking at her like that, but the truth is that I was. Front, back, side views; there wasn't one angle that I liked better than any other, for they were all downright splendid. If I'd had any Spanish or she knew any English . . .

I probably would've been too shy to say anything to her anyway. But I sure did a lot of looking and just as much thinking.

Mrs. Cardenas came out from the kitchen with the coffeepot. She stood there beside my table for a moment with the pot forgotten in her hand, looking first at her daughter and then transferring her smile to me. "Jou know what that silly girl says to me last night?" she asked.

"No, ma'am, I don't."

"Mama, no!" Juana shrieked, and began spraying frantic Spanish words into the air. I didn't know any Spanish, but I had no trouble figuring out the general gist of what she was saying. She didn't want mama talking to me, now that was for certain sure.

Mrs. Cardenas just laughed and ignored Juana, who dropped her scrub rag and came running over to grab her mother by the arm. "This girl last night, she says to me the big Anglo is the man she will marry."

"Mama!"

"Can you believe that, eh?" Mrs. Cardenas laughed. Juana turned red as a new bandanna. For that matter, I guess I did too. My cheeks and ears felt like furnaces with the fires stoked high. "Jus like that." She snapped her fingers. "One look at jou an' now she thinks of the wedding dress."

Juana burst into tears and fled. You'd think her mother would sympathize, but what she did was laugh and lean over to refill my coffee cup. Which didn't actually need refilling to begin with.

I was trying to decide if I should go after Juana myself, wondering if she would take it as comforting—which is what I would've intended—or as a response to what her mother had just said.

I'm not sure which I would have or, for that matter, should have done and never will find out, because just about the time Mrs. Cardenas turned back toward the kitchen the Arizona ranger came into the café. There were people I would rather have seen.

I tried to ignore him. Scooped up some of the soft, mashed beans on a piece of tortilla and popped it into my mouth.

The ranger came over and helped himself to a chair at my table without invitation. He was sitting directly across from me, and I noticed that he kept one hand beneath the table where I couldn't see.

Mrs. Cardenas said something and the ranger responded. Both of them in Spanish. He had told me this was Arizona, but you couldn't tell it by looking or by listening.

Whatever it was, she went away and came back moments later with another cup of coffee, a plate of puffy little pastries that looked like little bitty pillows and a dish of honey.

Mrs. Cardenas delivered the food and continued to stand there until the ranger said something to her. She gave him a dirty look and went back into the kitchen, leaving the two of us alone in the café.

The ranger waited until she was gone, then nodded toward the plate. He couldn't speak, I suppose, for he'd dredged one of the pastries into the honey and then stuffed the whole thing into his mouth.

"What are they?" I asked.

It took him a moment to chew and swallow before he could answer. And his right hand, I noted, had been out of sight the entire while. He was doing his eating left-handed. "Sopapillas," he said. "Try one. Best thing you've ever tasted. Count on it."

I did, mimicking him by putting honey all over one of the hot pastries—which turned out to be hollow, as I could tell once I picked it up—and sticking the whole dripping thing into my mouth.

"You might be right about that," I said after. "That's good."

"I'm always right," the ranger said. That was a joking declaration most times, but this guy said it like he meant it.

"I couldn't make that claim," I told him.

"I sent some wires off yesterday," he said.

"That's nice." I had another sopapilla. Darn but they were good.

"Got answers back this morning."

"Yes?"

"Have you heard of the Boyd Gang?"

I nodded. "Yes, I have. I ran into some fellows north of here a week or so ago. They said they were looking for somebody of that name. Did they catch them?"

"Not yet. But I think we're close. I got a description of the ringleader. He and his gang blew a safe in Lewisville Flats. They arrested him, but his gang busted him out of jail before they could try and hang the son of a bitch."

I resented being called that, never mind that the ranger thought it was justified.

"Then they blew another safe, this time in San Pablo City."

"I was there when that happened."

"Were you, now?"

"Yes, but I was standing in plain sight of half the town when we all heard the explosion. You can check with the town marshal there."

"I will too. The description the sheriff in Lewis County Nevada, gives me sounds an awful lot like you, Mr. Stewart."

"That's what the town marshal in San Pablo City told me, too. Mind if I have another one of your sopapillas, mister . . . What is your name, anyway?"

"Vaughn Maxwell," he said. "Help yourself to the sopapillas."

"They beat doughnuts hands down, don't they?"

"I've always thought so."

I was becoming uncomfortable from the way Ranger Maxwell kept staring at me. It was like he saw horns and a tail on me and thought that he was just the man to be tying a knot in the devil's tail.

Still, I forced myself to eat the sopapilla I'd asked for. Then I pushed my chair back and dug into my pocket. I brought out those four pennies and laid them beside my plate. The meal was free, but I expect a tip was in order anyhow.

I picked up my hat from the seat of the empty chair on my right and stood up. "Thanks for the . . . what was that thing again?" I remembered perfectly good and well what they were called, but I didn't think it would do any harm to redirect the direction this fellow's thoughts seemed to be running.

"Sopapilla," he said.

"Right. Thanks." I put my hat on, turned, and started out of there. I could feel a small trickle of sweat running down my ribs.

About the time I reached the door, the ranger called out to me.

"Hey, Boyd."

I'd been answering to that name my entire life.

I turned around toward him.

"Yeah, what?"

The words were no sooner out of my mouth than I felt the blood drain out of my stupid head.

I'd messed up.

Bad.

Chapter Sixteen

Oh, Lordy! The ranger's gun came into his hand and he reached around to a back pocket and brought out some steel manacles. Well, I knew what that was about. After all, this was a tune I'd danced to before now.

There was no sense in running. Even if I'd thought a great, hulking lummox like me could outrun a lean and fit fellow like Ranger Maxwell—which I didn't—there was no outrunning a .45 slug. And I didn't for a minute think he would hesitate to fire. There was a hardness in his eyes that told me I shouldn't take any chances with this one. He would shoot in a heartbeat and not think twice about it.

I sighed and put my hands up. Maxwell took a step forward.

And then had to brace himself against the tornado that came ripping out of the kitchen, yammering something in Spanish and throwing herself at the man like a rabid bobcat in a henhouse.

It was Juana, and I'd never seen any human person so overwrought as she was right then.

Her face was red as a train lantern. Tears were running

out of her eyes and snot out of her nose. She kept yelling curses in Spanish—believe me, I didn't have to understand the words to know what they were—and she actually, literally threw herself onto Maxwell like that same bobcat climbing a tall old tree.

Maxwell yanked his arm high to keep Juana from shooting herself or anybody else. With his free hand he tried to fend her off. Didn't have much success at it, but he tried. Juana was scaling him like he was a ladder. Trying to get up to where he was holding that gun. I suppose she wanted to snatch it away from him so I could run. Whatever her intention, she kept shouting "Michael, Michael, Michael" over and over again and tossing in some other stuff that I had no notion what it might've meant. Good advice, probably. Like "get the hell out of here now while you can."

Good advice, I'm sure, but I didn't take it. I was scared something would happen and Juana would get shot by accident. Better me than her. I stepped toward the ranger. He saw me coming and brought the gun down, ready to use it and never mind that Juana had his ear in her teeth. She couldn't talk while she was doing that, of course, but she sure could squeal like a shoat being picked up by its hind legs.

I shook my head and reached forward. I took hold of Juana and, gently as I could under the circumstances, pulled her off the ranger.

"Dammit!" he bawled in English, and then went into a spiel of Spanish that it is probably just as well I couldn't understand or I would've felt compelled to whack him one for using language like that in front of a lady.

Juana was crying so hard, I figured she was going to either shake herself to bits or drain out all her body fluids given another minute or two. I wrapped my arms tight around her and kept her from having another go at the ranger.

Maxwell seemed to feel he had things under control again, a little bit anyhow, and pulled a bandanna out of his pocket to mop up some of the blood that was running from the furrows Juana had gouged into his face and neck. And some of the sticky, stringy snot she'd left behind, too. He made a face when he saw that. But then, I would've done the same if it was me.

"Hold still, damn it," he snapped. Not that I'd been going anyplace. "And quit hiding behind her skirt." I turned loose of Juana. Then had to grab her again when she tried to go at Maxwell's throat one more time.

"Concepcion!" Maxwell bellowed, and a couple seconds later Mrs. Cardenas stuck her head in from the kitchen to see if it was safe to come in now. Maxwell said something to her in Spanish and she said something to Juana, and Juana began to tremble and cry harder than ever.

She pulled away from me and dropped down onto her knees and crawled on her knees over to Vaughn Maxwell's feet, blubbering and talking the whole way. Pitched herself facedown and clutched at his boots, begging and bawling and pleading like she was the one who was in for a hanging.

I couldn't . . . Lordy, I couldn't even *speak* with the girl. We didn't have the same language. We didn't come from the same culture or background. She was probably half my age.

And yet there she was, down on her knees begging Maxwell to let me be.

Which of course he did not.

He said something to Mrs. Cardenas, who came over and got down beside Juana and whispered to her and after a bit helped Juana onto her feet and out of the way so Maxwell was free to do what he had to do.

"Turn around," he told me, "and put your hands behind your back, Boyd. You know how. You've been there before."

I didn't say anything.

After all, what was there to say? He was right.

I turned around and put my hands behind my back.

Chapter Seventeen

"You," I blurted. "It was you I saw yesterday."

Liam O'Day was standing in the doorway there. He had a small brown bottle in his hand not unlike one of Professor Burdash's medicine bottles or else a half pint whiskey bottle with no label on it.

He held it up so we all could see. "Nitroglycerin," he announced. Which damn sure got my attention. Even Maxwell, tough ranger that he was, seemed to turn a little pale when he heard that.

I don't know all that much about nitro. But I was guessing that half a pint of the stuff could raze the building this café was in and have some punch left over to mess up the neighbors, too.

"What we're gonna do here, lads an' lassies, is all of us stand nice an' still. Exceptin' for me old pal Boyd here. He'll be takin' a wee trip while the rest of us stay put, if y' take me meaning."

"Liam, what are you doing here?" I demanded.

"Not now, boyo. We've an escape t' be makin', don't you see."

251

"No, damn it, I want to know. What are you doing here?"

Liam laughed. And held the nitro bottle high, as if it were a charm that would ward off Arizona rangers. Actually, it may have been. Certainly worked like one, anyhow. "Why, laddy, I been following you, not wantin' you t' make any the more trouble for y'sel', d'you see."

"Foll . . . Liam, I've been following *you*!"

He chuckled. "Not since San Pablo, ye haven't."

"But—"

"That fool posse that caught you shoulda caught the both o' us, boyo. They were so intent on sneakin' up on you they walked right past me." He laughed loudly. "One o' them s' close I coulda reached out an' touched his pantleg when he went by, would ye b'lieve it."

With Liam I think I would have believed anything.

"An' now here we be. An' there this fine, upstandin' officer o' the law be. Say na . . . I see it's a gun ye have in yer hand there. Be a good lad, will ye, an' put the rascally thing away. Guns make me nervous, don't ya know, an' 't wouldna do for me to be droppin' this wee bottle." He puffed his cheeks out, then made a loud noise. "Just like that. Poof. We're all naught but splinters and wet bits."

I really think that until that moment Maxwell had forgotten he still had that revolver in his hand. Now that Liam reminded him Maxwell peered at it, then at us, then down at the gun again.

His expression hardened, and he pointed the gun at Liam. "Drop that bottle, bud, or I'll shoot you where you stand."

"Aye, an' if ye do, lad, it's all of us will fly with the birdies. Do you drop me, I drop this. An' if I drop this, we're all blown t' smithereens, d'you see."

Maxwell went pale again. He held the gun. But he sure couldn't use it.

Over by the kitchen door Mrs. Cardenas whispered something to Juana, who obviously had been missing out on most of what was going on here. Mrs. Cardenas took Juana by the shoulders and tried to hasten her away.

Juana was having none of it. She tore loose from her mama and ran to grab tight onto me, throwing her arms around me and clinging to me tight as a tick in a dog's ear. She said something to her mother, her voice hot and determined.

"I'll be damned," Maxwell declared.

I couldn't have put it better myself. I didn't need the words to understand that Juana had decided if I was going to be blown up she would stand there and be blown up with me.

I didn't . . . good Lord, I'd never so much as touched the girl until right this moment. Well, except for when I dragged her off the ranger a few minutes before. Still couldn't talk with her, though.

I guess when Juana made up her mind about something she meant it. Even that crazy declaration she'd made to her mother the night before.

It was powerfully affecting to see and to feel the completeness of what she was offering to me, though. It was more than I'd known one person was capable of giving to another.

I put my arm around her and bent down to give her a light kiss on the forehead. "Would somebody please tell Juana that everything is going to be all right," I said.

Both Mrs. Cardenas and Ranger Maxwell spoke to her.

"Ask her to go outside," I said. "Out back. I'll let her know where she can come meet me later on."

Again both of them spoke with her, then Mrs. Cardenas said, "She does not believe jou."

"I promise," I said, tipping Juana's chin up so I could look her in the eyes when I said it, even though the words had to be filtered through her mama.

She reached up to grasp my wrist in both her hands. Then she smiled and stepped back, holding on to me until she was too far away and finally had to let go. She turned and ran out into the kitchen, out of sight.

Mrs. Cardenas wasn't half a second behind her, leaving just us three menfolk still in the café.

"Boyd, lad," Liam said.

"Yes?"

"Get on yer horse, old son, an' ride for Mexico. It's naught but two mile south o' here."

"Two miles," I groaned.

"Aye. Funny, innit. I'll gi' ye time t' make half the run an' then I'll be comin' lickety-split behind. Ye got that na?"

"I do," I told him.

"An' while you're out enjoyin' yer wee commune wi' Nature, lad, me an' my new friend will stand here an' contemplate the wonders o' chemistry in this modern era."

Liam laughed so hard, he doubled over and held his belly.

With the same hand that also held the nitro bottle.

"Jayzus!" Liam barked.

And the bottle slipped out of his grasp to plummet toward the floor.

Chapter Eighteen

I cringed, tightening every muscle I knew I had and a bunch that were previously unsuspected as well.

"Juana," I cried out. "I'm sorry."

My words were partially drowned out by the sound of breaking glass.

The room was quickly filled. With the hot smell of whiskey.

"*Run, Boyd!*" Liam shouted. And instantly followed his own advice.

He spun around and went dashing out the front door into the street.

Vaughn Maxwell was just as quick. And Maxwell had the revolver still in his hand.

Before I realized what the ranger was up to, before I had a chance to jump him, he lifted his gun and took brief aim, then fired.

Liam cried out and went down face forward onto the hard earth, a hole shot in his back and the bright blood already soaking his shirt before I could get to his side.

I dropped to my knees and pulled the little man into my

lap. "Damn you. Damn you," I kept shouting at Maxwell, who stood there with no remorse, the gun in one hand and manacles in the other.

Juana was there too. I hadn't seen where she came from, but she was there. She kept saying something. I knew, of course. It was a relief that the bullet was meant for Liam and not for me.

As for myself, well, I wasn't so sure.

Men began to appear on the sidewalks and inch tentatively into the street. Maxwell, after all, was the one who was still standing.

"Move aside," a gruff voice ordered. "Move aside." A bald man wearing a barber's apron pushed me out of the way to take over with Liam, ripping Liam's shirt open and using the tail of the shirt to try to stanch the bleeding.

Maxwell motioned with the muzzle of his .45 and I stood. I took time to give Juana an all-too-brief hug, then turned and put my hands behind my back while Maxwell clamped the irons painfully tight on my wrists.

Maxwell took me by one elbow and Juana grabbed tight onto the other—with those manacles in place that hurt like hell, but I wasn't about to tell her that—and in that manner the three of us walked down the street to the Los Palomitos jail.

Chapter Nineteen

I sat on the edge of a hard bunk—wood this time, not so fancy as the steel bunks back in the Lewis County, Nevada, jail—and I waited.

Patience is one of the first lessons of jail life. I'd learned that. Now I was given another opportunity to exercise the knowledge.

Beyond the barred window the sun was sinking rapidly toward a chain of very distant mountains.

It had been . . . what?—three weeks now since Liam was shot. Long weeks.

They said there was some argument as to which trial would be held first, the one here in Arizona at San Pablo City or the one across the line into Nevada at Lewisville Flats. I didn't really much care which it was. One would be about as bad as the other.

Except that wasn't really so. It was only in Nevada where they insisted on pressing charges that would make it a capital case with hanging as a possible outcome. Here in Arizona they told me the maximum sentence for blowing the San Pablo bank safe wouldn't be more than twenty, perhaps twenty-five years tops. I wasn't sure if that would beat hanging or not.

"Hello," a voice whispered.

"Hello yourself. You went away for a little while there."

"Aye, it's a lazy lout that I be, boyo. Always have been. It's why I turned to a life o' crime, don't y' see. Easier than workin' for me brass."

I smiled at him. Crazy little son of a bitch. Back in San Pablo—he had a receipt to prove it or I'd have been sure he was lying—he first went to the bank to send off a letter of credit. To my uncle Edward. It was only after Uncle Edward's horse money was safely on its way that he blew the bank safe and robbed back much of the gold he'd left there.

"Don't y' see, lad, I didna know at th' time would I be seein' y' again," he'd told me. "Besides, I was wantin' t' sell that great lump of a harse o' yours an' the saddle too. Too heavy fer the likes o' me what wi' all that gold inside, which th' weight told me first off, an' the seat o' that saddle 'way too big for my wee backside."

He really had sent Uncle Edward's horse money back to my home in Nevada. And when I'd asked him why, he gave me a wounded look and said, "But lad. It's friends we are, innit? D'ye think I would steal from a friend? Nay, lad."

And then he'd laughed. "D'you hear 'ow much the Boyd Gang made off with from San Pablo, lad?"

"Of course. Eleven thousand something."

Liam only laughed again. " 'Twas not a copper more than eighteen hundred, boyo. An' in Nevada they reported seventeen thousand t' the insurance comp'ny while I only nicked 'em for a bit more'n three. Now tell me, old son. Which o' us would ye say is the greater thief?"

"Liam," I told him again this evening, "I don't know how to thank you."

He waved the thanks away. As he did every time I brought it up. "What else would a friend do for a friend, eh?" And he laughed. "Even if 'twasn't true, although in this case it be the truth, the whole truth an' nothin' but the truth. Mostly."

The thing was, back in the street when we'd all thought